# The

# MILLIONAIRE

# MISTRESS

*Cooper*

## By TIPHANI MONTGOMERY

A Life Changing Book *in conjunction with* Power Play Media
**Published by Life Changing Books**
P. O. Box 423 Brandywine, MD 20613

*www.lifechangingbooks.net*

*Library of Congress Cataloging-in-Publication Data; 200693647*

ISBN 10 digit 0-9741394-6-7
ISBN 13 digit 978-0-974-13946-3
*Copyright ® 2006*

*This book is dedicated to my mother*

*Brenda "Peggy" Joyce Rodriguez Montgomery Ellison*

*HAPPY FATHER'S DAY*

# ACKNOWLEDGMENTS

You never know how many people you actually know until you have to sit down and thank them for whatever contribution they've made in your life. There are so many people that I want to thank, I'm afraid that I won't remember them all. To the friend that gave me a smile and words of encouragement when I was sure I couldn't go on, I say thank you. To everyone I have forgotten, please forgive me. I hope you know that all you've done (or haven't done) in my life is appreciated. It's only made me stronger.

Some acknowledgements are longer than others. To the people that felt like theirs should've been stronger, it is in my heart.

To my God, words can't express my gratitude for the gift of writing that you've given me. I've wandered away from Your will in my life too many times, but your grace and mercy have kept me from harm. You ordered my steps even when I ran away from You, most of the time tripping and falling, so I say thank You. I ask your forgiveness for being a part time Christian and your wisdom to guide me through what is to come next. With you by my side, I can't fail.

To my beautiful mother Brenda. You are the best example God could've given me, and I'm sorry for not telling you that enough. Great mothers aren't born, they're molded and shaped by their trials and tribulations to become what their children need them to be. You are one person that this world is blessed to have and I love you. To my sister Carrie, "Yah Yah" Montgomery, thanks for being my number one cheerleader when I needed it the most. You are still the world's best sister. To my daughter Jaedah Kiss, I love you so much. It's been a long six years and I wouldn't trade it in for the world. I still can't believe I'm somebody's mother. Thank you for screening my calls when I was writing so I wouldn't be disturbed, you took that job so seriously.

To my mom #2- Pam Evans Montgomery, my brothers T-Tom Evans, and Cyrus "Spunge" Procter, I did it again! I love ya'll from the bottom of my heart. To Renee and Nate Cole, thank you both for all that you've done. The sacrifice that you made for Jaedah and I will never be forgotten.

To my brother and sister Tex and Chey (King and Queen of NC), can you believe it? I told you both from the beginning that I was going to make it big and look at me now. This is nothing compared to the vision I have for my future and I have you to thank. Both of you took your time to upgrade me into the woman I am today, and even though I have a long way to go, I'm definitely on the right track. I love you both dearly and I'm thankful that you're in my life.

They say blessings come in disguises; Tonya Ridley (The Takeover) you were without a doubt definitely one of them. I had been writing all my life, mostly poetry, but you were the one that gave me the courage to write a novel. Before I even had a deal, you spoke words of encouragement as if I had already made it. Then, when I signed my contract, you talked to me about what would be next when my book hit number one. You took time out of your busy schedule to help me and frequently cursed me out, but it was all worth it!

To Azarel, thank you for accepting my project. It all happened so fast, I'm not sure where the time went. I

*v*

remember one of the many late nights when I called you panicking. I had just written six chapters of my book, walked away from the computer for a couple of minutes and when I sat back down, everything was gone. You sat on the phone with me calmly while I frantically searched for a document that was never recovered. Instead of giving up, I picked my face up off the ground and didn't go back to sleep until everything was written again. This is going to be a hit, and I'm ready for the next one! I wish you and your family many blessings.

To my publicist Nakea, thank you for pushing this book to come out way sooner than it was supposed to. You're a beast in this game and I'm blessed to have you on my side. I can't wait to read yours soon. Thank you! To all of the professionals who worked on this project, Leslie Allen, Kathleen Jackson, Brian Holscher, and Davida Baldwin, I thank you from the bottom of my heart. The three of you worked extremely hard on this project and I appreciate your hard work. To my test readers, Cheryl Duckett Moody, Tonya Ridley, Tamara Cooke, Catina Brooks, and Keisha George( Poole Road), I am sooooooo grateful for your honesty. A special thanks to Kiesha. Where do I start? You had no reason to help me as unselfishly as you did, determining to make this book a success. I called you all times of night and you always stopped what you were doing to make sure I was on the right track. There were times when I had read it so much that nothing seemed to make sense and you assured me that this was a great book. You always knew when I was at my limit and you smothered me with positive words and great ideas. Thank you.

To my entire Power Play/Life Changing Books Family-Danette Majette (I Shoulda Seen it Comin), Darren Coleman (Ladies Listen Up, Don't Ever Wonder), J.Tremble (Secrets of a Housewife, More Secrets More Lies), Tonya Ridley (The Take Over), Tyrone Wallace (Nothin' Personal), Mike G (Young Assassin), and Azarel (Bruised, A Life to Remember); just wanted to give you all a big shot out!

To everyone that picks up the book and looks at the cover, for the last time, that is not me! I like to give a big thanks to Kim Pae (www.kimpae.com) for blessing me with that banging cover! I'm a holla at you about the movie.

To the Supper Clubb family, Uncle E (aka Ninja Roach), stop looking at me crazy when I ask you questions. I just be wantin' to know! Uncle Pete, Shameek, Samzelle (he sounds like a great guy), Moe Vega, Kat, El, thank ya'll for all the support and love.

To my friends Marla Dinkle, Khara "Sweet Muffins" Grant, Karza "Friend" Walton, Yolanda "Pooh" Richardson, Shaunita "Skinny" Randolph, and Mitch Summerfield, I love you all unconditionally.

To my cousins Shameika "Goldie" Moore, Bridget Johnson, Shawn and Juan Yarborough, Wally and Brandon Evans, Stan Evans (I wish you'd stay your ass out of jail), and to all the rest, I love ya'll. Big shout out to Shawkz Entertainment.

To City in The South Records, Bow Boa and Sunrise, I'll see ya'll at the top! Big shout out to DJ Deluxe and the south's best kept secret DJ Skillz, for showing me love. I wish ya'll the best in everything you do. To Control (Rob and Steele), this book was out of control. I have no doubt that you'll blow up in this industry. Thanks to Young (BK) for the frequent check up calls, I appreciated all of them. To Charlamagne the God (still bustin them stupid dope moves) thanks for all the love. Thanks to Azeah for building my Website. It's on fire! To Markita Finkley, thank you for taking the time out to read my book. I appreciated the advice.

I was born and raised in Rochester, NY and I rep it everywhere I go. I'm proud to be where I'm from, and I thank everybody there in advance for all the love. WDKX (103.9) is still going strong. To all the blocks Hudson, North Clinton, Thurston, Genesee St, North St, etc. keep your heads up. Too many of ya'll are dying for nothing, it's time for a change. Big shout out to Lost Boro Entertainment, June your time is now!

I moved to NC when I was 21 and I've been here ever since. It ain't as slow as people may think. To Raleigh's south side, I got mad love for ya'll. Thank you for everything. Ya'll are the reason I sold over 2,000 copies of my poetry book, Hate Me Bitch! Lil B, keep your head up! To the Bull City (Durham), Port City (Wilmington), Charlotte and the surrounding areas, thank you! In the short time that I've been here, too many of my niggas have gotten life sentences. To my home girl Latoya Lee, I haven't forgotten about you. Keep your head up. To my nigga Country, I wish that they'd just let you out for one night so that you can hang with us. We'd bring you back. Shit always happens to good people but you'll survive. At the end of the day, all that shit wasn't worth the rest of your lives. I only pray that someone else learns from your mistakes.

To my God sister Ashlyn Boler, Trina Hill, and Gail and

Pam Evans, thanks for everything. To my Dad, where are you?

I hope I'm not forgetting anyone but I have a strong feeling I am. Again please accept my apologies.

They said I wouldn't make it. I had my daughter when I was eighteen and most had already planned my downfall, but God had different plans. I barley made it past high school and went to college sometimes. I wasn't stupid, just smart enough to know that a little hustle in me was greater than a piece of paper with a degree on it. I WILL MAKE IT TO THE TOP!! To single mothers out there who don't think that they can make it, remember that with God by your side, all things are possible. I am a living witness, and so are the people I surround my self with. Look at the company you keep and decide today to make a change. Everyone is not going to be happy about your new take on life but with success breeds envy. I only advise you to be prepared.

Please send all comments to www.tiphani.net and visit me at myspace.com/tiphanitheauthor or www.lifechangingbooks.net to post your comment about the book on the site. I'd love to hear your thoughts.

Holla,
Tiphani Montgomery
IT'S THE ROC!

# 1

# OSHYN

## (2001)

"Where the fuck have you been?" I asked Trent, smelling his funky weed from across the room.

He immediately ducked from the cordless phone that was flying straight toward his head. It only missed because of my swollen eyes. I had been crying the ugly cry.

"Bitch, don't question me. Your young ass needs to play your position, and be lucky I'm still taking care of you!"

"Oh, so now I'm a young bitch? I'm eighteen years old and eight months pregnant with your son and I'm a bitch? Two fucking days, Trent! You been gone for two fucking days, and you couldn't even call to let me know that you were okay?" I stood with my hands below my protruding belly, ready to slice his ass. "You come walking in here at nine o'clock in the morning after being missing in action, and I'm a bitch? When did it get like this? What did I do to deserve being treated like shit?" I asked, crying like a little baby. I promised myself I wouldn't get soft, at least not this time. I couldn't help it though, my feelings were torn apart. "When did you stop loving me?" I screamed.

Silence.

Dead silence.

I stared at the man who used to love me. The man whose six-two frame used to smother me with hugs after a long day of getting money. The man who loved to sit between my legs and kiss my thighs, while I braided his long thick hair. I looked at the gold fronts on the bottom of his teeth, which enhanced his already perfect smile, remembering how sexy he used to make me feel. Trent looked a little different now — same body, different soul.

I wish I had a sixth sense so I could figure out exactly what was wrong with him. Him staying out all night was becoming all too familiar. I guess in a way, part of me was in denial. I watched him ignore me as I stared off into space. *Maybe reminiscing about the past would bring back some good memories*, I thought.

It's funny how your life turns out, because I didn't like Trent when we first met two years ago. We were at Rush Henrietta's High School basketball tournament. He was a twenty year old, well-known dope boy and stick-up kid, known for having money and a flashy lifestyle, but I wasn't impressed. Most of the people I hung around were guys, and I knew about all the games they played with the countless bitches they chased. None of my homeboys were worth shit, and they didn't want anything more than some pussy or head from whatever groupie willing to give it to them.

To me, Trent wasn't different, but he was annoyingly persistent. He had a little dough, and word on the street was that he snatched up any chick that crossed his path. It was out of character for him to have someone like me brushing him off. He was used to bitches dropping their panties at the drop of a dime, but not me. I wasn't interested in being added to the, *I fucked her club.*

He was persistent as hell. I remember days when Trent would wait for me at my bus stop with dozens of red roses and fluffy teddy bears. At first, I was hesitant, but eventually I accepted the roses, stuffed animals, and the other gifts that followed.

"Why don't you just leave me alone?" I finally asked one day, aggravated at his constant uninvited presence. To the on-lookers, he was just a sweet guy trying to treat me nice, but I knew the truth; boys were all the same. He wanted something in return for all the gifts he'd gotten me, and it was most likely pussy. I was one of the few virgins left in my school, and I wasn't going to ruin my reputation by giving up some ass.

Trent begged to take me out, promising that if I didn't enjoy myself he would leave me alone for good. That was an offer too good to refuse, so I agreed to the one date, and since then we were inseparable. Not once did he try to fuck or disrespect me in any way. It wasn't until a few months later that I decided to give him what I cherished the most, my virginity.

Sex with Trent was everything a girl could imagine. His gentle touch and delicate stroke had me hooked. He knew exactly how to make me feel good and I loved every minute of it. I guess that's why after I found out about my pregnancy, my excitement was uncontrollable. I knew at that point, I had him for life.

While we were pillow talking one night, Trent told me that he knocked me up on purpose. Surprisingly to him, I didn't get upset. The smile on my face widened and I jumped into his arms without hesitation. The fact that we would be a family had me happier than a faggot with a dick in his mouth.

On occasions, he would always tell me how much he cared for me, and that he wanted me to have his son, be his wife, and raise his family. I believed him and had no doubt that he'd be a good father to his children. Trent vowed to raise our kids better than his crackhead parents. He had five sisters and one brother; all younger and still living in the foster care system. He hated his mother for that. Maybe that's why he insisted on serving her when the monkey on her back came scratching.

I asked him once, why he insisted on giving his mother the drugs. That was after I watched her deteriorating body thank him for the poison that ran through her veins daily. I told him that he needed to help her. My suggestion was to admit her into rehab and not condone her habit any longer. I tried putting myself in his shoes, but just couldn't see doing that to my mother.

Trent snapped, with a little hostility in his voice, saying that he would rather give drugs to her for free than to wonder which one of his homeboys she fucked or sucked to get her fix. He also made it clear to never question him again about his mother. I left the subject alone, still feeling crazy about the whole idea of him serving his mother, but realized that his back was against the wall with very little options. Deep down inside, I think he wanted to be responsible for her slow death.

When we talked about the pregnancy, Trent informed me that Steve, his best friend, would be the godfather. Steve and Trent grew up together on the east side of Rochester, New York. They were closer than brothers, the only family each other had ever known. When I was four months pregnant, Steve went missing. His girlfriend called Trent when he didn't come home from a run. Trent immediately knew something was seriously wrong. In Rochester, New York, hustling and coming up missing only meant one thing...death.

Trent searched and searched, and asked questions from Rochester to Harlem. Two months later, Steve's body was found decapitated inside of a plastic bag at the bottom of the Genesee River. Some said it was the mob, others said it was a stick-up gone wrong, but no matter what happened that night, Trent hadn't been right ever since.

His behavior mocked that of a person whose weed had been laced with angel dust. His mind was gone. Then the rumors came. It seemed this nigga just couldn't keep his dick in his pants. He was never satisfied. I ended up cutting a couple of bitches up over him. With my son in my stomach, I foolishly fought over dick that wasn't mine. Apparently never was.

I recalled a time when I was five months pregnant. I asked Trent if he wanted to go to the movies to get his mind off of Steve. He hadn't been social, and I wanted us to spend a little more time together. He brushed me off, saying that he was busy and needed to make a run. I was hurt as hell when he strutted out the door, leaving a trail of his old-ass Cool Water scented cologne behind. Things seemed suspicious, but I couldn't pinpoint anything.

I yelled as the door shut in my face, "Don't forget my food!"

That night I decided to stay in and take some time for myself. My cell phone rang a few times, but I ignored it. My instinct told me it was Trent so I decided to check the caller ID. I saw that it was my homegirl, Apples, so I quickly answered the phone.

Before I could say hello, she unloaded all the details of her spotting Trent and some light-skinned bitch that went to Franklin High School at the movies. She said everybody saw them hugged up and kissing all over each other. I was sick to my stomach! *I asked that motherfucker to go with me to the movies, and he's there with some bitch*! I could hear Apples hyperventilating through the phone. She acted as if Trent was her man. The next thing I knew, she told me to get ready, she was on the way to my house.

I hurried when her words, "If we hustle, we can catch them as they come out the theatre," registered.

I remember hanging up the phone, still shocked at what I had just heard. *But he was supposed to be on the way home with my Country Sweet Chicken*, I thought, wondering why he would do something like that to me. His actions answered a lot of things, though. Trent hadn't touched me in a while, and maybe a new woman was why. He had gotten another bitch and was slowly kicking me out of his life, but I wasn't going without a fight.

Apples pulled up to the crib, and we made it back to the movies in record time. We cased the parking lot, making sure Trent's burgundy Tahoe was still there. We spotted his truck, parked in the cut, and watched like two detectives on a stake-out. I rubbed my hands nervously around my belly, wishing my baby could comfort me. An hour passed and there still was no sign of Trent, or his bitch. I banged my fist on the dash.

"Damn, what the fuck did they go see?" I shouted.

Apples said nothing. She was ready for war. Just as

she pulled out the Vaseline, we finally noticed a group of people walking out the theater. I thought my eyes were deceiving me when I saw Trent with his hands wrapped around some chick's shoulders. He had a big smile on his face, something that I hadn't seen in a while.

I jumped out the car like Rambo, and ran straight toward them. Not saying a word, I swung, cutting the bitch in the face with my box cutter. She didn't have any idea who I was, and she definitely didn't know what I cut her with. Trent was shocked. He looked like he wanted to run for help, but instead his eyes stayed glued on me. I'm not sure if it was because of all the blood that was squirting out of her face, or because he had been caught. Maybe it was a combination of both, but either way, the nigga quickly removed his arm, as she fell to the ground holding her face.

Trent opened his mouth to justify himself, and before he could utter an explanation, I swung the blood covered box cutter toward his face, barely missing it. Before I knew it, his punk ass was screaming like a bitch. His right hand had been split wide open, and I didn't give a fuck.

My young mind couldn't comprehend why any of that happened to me. I was a model girlfriend, didn't hang out, cooked, cleaned, and did my best to keep him satisfied. I even moved out of my Grandma's crib and in with him once I got pregnant.

Although Trent forgave me after the incident at the

movies, our relationship was never the same. Just when I thought things would get better, Trent eventually started coming home later and sometimes not at all. I was tired of being treated like the other woman, and decided to stand my ground.

When I questioned him about his late hours, he'd get verbally abusive and threaten to leave me, but today was different. I didn't give a fuck what happened. I was sick of being treated like shit, sick of being neglected. *This can't be what love is about*, I reasoned with myself, thinking this wasn't the man I met two years ago. I was determined to put an end to his madness.

"Trent," I said, bringing myself back to reality. I had done so much reflecting, that I forgot I'd asked him a question. "I asked you when did you stop loving me?" I repeated, as if he hadn't heard me the first time.

Still no answer.

He made himself comfortable at the kitchen table, pretending to be busier than he really was, counting out the money scattered around the money machine.

"Where the fuck you been?" I screamed, frustrated that he was ignoring me. I knocked the neatly placed stacks of one hundred dollar bills off the table. The dirty money fluttered everywhere, hitting us in the face as it landed. There was a light scent of currency in the air that I hated. I didn't know if it was because of the pregnancy, but I could smell everything, especially dirty money.

"You stupid bitch!" Trent yelled.

I flinched from his deformed hand that was raised in the air; the hand that I marked for life. Trent had never hit me before, even when I stabbed him. I guess he realized what he was doing and put his hand back down.

"Stop asking me all these stupid ass questions, Oshyn," he said, while walking away from the table. "Now have this shit picked up, some food on my table, and your pussy ready when I get out the shower!" he demanded.

*So much for being hard,* I thought to myself.

Thoughts of leaving Trent entered my mind, but I loved him. He was all I had ever known. He was my first, my last, my everything, as Barry White would say. I thought this was how a relationship was supposed to go.

I put my long hair into a ponytail because it kept sticking to my tear stained face. My round belly and weak heart didn't allow for easy bending, so I took my time picking up the mess I made when his cell phone rang. At that point, I was frustrated and definitely didn't want Trent to leave out for a run. I was ready to hide the phone until I glanced at the caller ID.

"Hello?" I answered quickly, wanting to know who Chocolate was.

"Is this Oshyn?" she asked, with a nasty attitude. I knew where this was headed. I'd had these conversations before — different bitch, same topic.

"Who the fuck is this?" I barked.

"This is Chocolate and I want to let you know that

Trent is my man, and I'm pregnant with his baby bitch, so you need to stop calling him in the middle of the night so that we can get some sleep!"

"Who the fuck you think you talking too? You can't know who I am!" I said, hitting her back with a question. Anyone who knew my M.O. wouldn't dare step to me with this bullshit, especially over this nigga. I'd kill a bitch over his dick. "Where you at bitch? I'm coming to see you!"

"I'm at 521 N. Clinton Avenue," she said, almost daring me to come.

This dumb broad actually lived on my side of town. "I'm on my way!" I shouted. After hanging up the phone, I considered asking Trent who Chocolate was, but chose not to, considering how our conversation just ended. Going to her crib was a must. I was too furious not to go. Besides, she probably had information that would satisfy some of my unanswered questions. I hated the thought of going out into the freezing cold, but this was crucial.

I threw on my black North Face coat, Timberlands and oversized mittens, and snuck out the crib. I ran up the street to the corner store and, just my luck, a cab was sitting there waiting for a fare. He took me to Chocolate's house, and I paid him a little extra to wait just in case something popped off.

I arrived at the spot, raced to the door, and started kicking it as hard as I could.

"Come out, bitch!" I screamed at the top of my lungs, hoping that she heard me. I kicked the door harder, leaving a slight dent on the aging wood. It finally opened.

She was short, struggling to even be five-two, and chunky. Her wavy red hair touched her wide waist and protruding stomach that confirmed her accusations of being pregnant. The bitch was huge and her nose was quite scary. Yeah, she was pregnant for real.

"What's up now?" she asked, pointing her chubby fingers in my face.

That was the biggest mistake she could have ever made. I never talked, just swung. I spit out my razor like a professional blade slinger and slashed her face wide open from her eyebrow to her cheek. Chocolate's flesh split wide open and blood gushed everywhere. She fell to her knees on the wooden porch and screamed in agony, while trying to hold her face together. No one heard us, and if they did, they didn't care. These were the sounds that we were use to in the hood, and it was music to everyone's ears compared to random gunshots.

I kicked her in the stomach multiple times with my Timbs, until I could barely breathe. I glanced behind me to make sure no one was watching. With all of my might, I turned around and hit her one last time.

"Don't call Trent's fucking phone again!" I demanded, still gasping for air. My chest heaved in and out heavily, as I walked back to the cab.

I was back to the crib in less than twenty minutes flat. I barged in the house with my hand caressing my cramping stomach screaming to the top of my lungs.

"Trent! Who the fuck is Chocolate…Trrreennttt!"

"Shut the fuck up with all that screaming!" he said, walking from the bedroom to the front door. He paused and looked at me. His dark eyes examined my trembling body. He blurted out, like he was pissed at me, "Where the fuck have you been? Why you got blood all over you?"

"Oh, now you want to know where I've been! Don't question me, you bitch ass nigga, after you knocked another bitch up! Let's see if you can look in her sliced up face while you fuck her now, you bitch ass…"
WHOP!

Trent rocked me in the face with his fist. He then walked into our bedroom, grabbed a handful of clothes, and threw them out the front door. I panicked, realizing the clothes belonged to me.

"Get the fuck out my house!" he yelled, with his fingers pointing to the dark street.

The door was wide open and I could feel the strong chill. "But where am I supposed to go?" I asked, turning my anger into tears. While I tasted the blood that trickled into my mouth, my heart sank. "What about our baby?"

"I don't even know if it's mine, bitch. Beat it!"

With that, he pushed me out the house and slammed

the door. The thunderous sound of the door closing in my face, echoed through my ears, making my headache much more painful.

It hurt so bad, I could barely breathe. Why would he even question the paternity of our child? I cried like a baby on the steps, scared to move. I couldn't understand why I was sitting outside our house, eight months pregnant in December.

"AAAHHHHHHHHH!" I screamed, balled over in pain. The cramping in my stomach had gotten worse, and the thought of losing my baby, had me terrified. "Trent, let me in! Something isn't right!" I screamed, holding my stomach tightly. With the little energy left in me, I pounded on the door like the police. Something was definitely wrong, because the pain was almost unbearable. "Trent, please help me," I said, in between gasps for air.

The pain was hitting me once every few minutes, so I couldn't walk for help. I sat, shivering on the front porch, waiting for Trent to come to his senses. I felt my stomach switch positions, no longer sitting high, where it once was.

"AAAAAHHHHH!" I wailed again, at the top of my lungs. The pain knocked me down to the ground, where I ended up stretched out in the snow. I just laid there, freezing. There was no way that I could move. The pain was absolutely paralyzing.

I blacked out.

I woke up on a stretcher, getting ready to be lifted into the ambulance. The red-head female paramedic told me that my neighbor saw me laid out in the snow. He knew I was pregnant and called for help.

"Good thing he did," she said, in her soft nurturing voice. "Your water broke and your contractions are a minute apart." She took a moment and softly moved my frizzy hair out of my face. "We've checked your skin and there aren't any punctured wounds anywhere…whose blood is this? What happened? Is someone else hurt?"

I ignored the freckled-face lady who was only there to help, and laid on the stretcher, feeling like I was near death. My body was numb, probably from being covered in the snow.

I stared at the house that was once my home and noticed Trent staring out our bedroom window. Our eyes met. I mouthed, "Why?"

He looked at me with a cold pair of eyes. I turned my head slightly, hoping that my eyes were deceiving me. I could've sworn he mouthed FUCK YOU. He closed the curtain and I never saw him again.

My introduction to love had left me for dead.

# 2

# CHLOE

## (2001)

"FUCK!" Trent moaned, as I slid his big dick as far back into my throat as it would allow. I brought my pace back to a moderate speed and massaged his dick inside my warm mouth.

To him it felt like good, wet pussy. The end was coming near. I always knew because he started fucking my face. I sucked faster, like I was trying to break the dick sucking record of the year. Out of the blue, Trent nutted in my mouth and I massaged his balls until he begged for mercy.

"Damn Chloe! You trying to suck a nigga dry?" he said, struggling to catch his breath.

I sat back on my Grandmother's queen-sized bed and smiled, admiring my gifted talents. *If she knew that I was in her room...on her bed, she would kill me.* I thought about the consequences I would have to deal with if Grandma found out what I was doing in her room. My bed, a twin, was way too small to handle my activities, so I used hers every chance I got.

Trent's loud cell phone, singing on the old wooden nightstand, interrupted my daydreaming.

"Yeah, what up?" he asked the caller, while I kissed his damp face. "On the news? Fuck!" His body tensed up and his body language changed. "Chloe, go turn on the news," he ordered.

I crawled, on all fours seductively, to the edge of the bed and turned the channel to the news. My cousin, Oshyn, was on the screen being put on a stretcher and into the ambulance in the middle of a snowstorm. The reporter said that last night Oshyn's neighbor found her lying on a bed of snow in the front yard, balled up in fetal position with blood all over her. The neighbor also told the nosey news reporter that he thought Oshyn was dead and was relieved to learn that she had only passed out.

Trent got off the phone and sat up straight. I watched his facial expression change. I could tell he was stressed. He lowered his head and rubbed his temple in an attempt to rid his guilty conscious. He knew he was fucked up, but he looked damn good with his rock-hard chest, and semi-hard dick, still looking at me.

"You never told me what happened last night. Why did you just leave her out there like that?" I asked him, not really concerned with Oshyn's well being. I just wanted to know his motive. My grandmother had already told me bits and pieces about what happened, but I wanted the story straight from the horse's mouth.

He shrugged his shoulders and shook his head.

"My grandma told me that she had the baby as soon as she got to the hospital last night. She named your son, Micah."

I knew he loved her, but he played it off like he didn't even care. I knew his fine ass hadn't been right ever since his boy Steve got killed, but damn he was a new father. It was like someone had ripped his heart out of his chest and told him to keep living.

I crawled back to the television and turned it off. Too many times, Oshyn had gotten too much attention.

"Look, that was last night and this is a brand new day." I got off the bed and floated across the room to my grandmother's old stereo system. I started up my R. Kelly baby making mix CD, and headed back to my dick. As I seductively danced toward him, I caught a glimpse of myself in the cherry wood mirror.

*Damn, I hate sounding conceited, but I know why Trent is here with me,* I thought to myself, admiring my hourglass shape. My 36 C cups sat up perfectly, and my ass was simply big and round with no cellulite or dimples in sight. I knew a lot of nineteen year olds that have already let themselves go, but not me. I took care of my body, because it made me a lot of money. My sun kissed skin was tight and flawless. My jet-black hair, a little ruffled, fell to the middle of my back, making me the envy of most of these baldheaded bitches in my hood. I forced myself to part from the mirror and crawled back on the bed to finish what I had started.

"Baby, come over here. We gotta hurry up before my grandma gets home," I said, in an attempt to get him back in the mood again so I could get my money.

He hit me off with three hundred dollars every time we fucked, which was about four times out the week. I didn't have a job, nor did I want one, and Trent paid well. I figured this had to last me for at least another two years, until I turned twenty-one and could get my mother's life insurance policy, which was five hundred thousand dollars. I hadn't even gotten the money yet and knew exactly what I was going to do with it. Live the life I was supposed to live, the life of luxury.

I already saw myself vacationing in Tahiti, taking on the world's best ski slopes in Denver, and traveling all over the world, tasting the finest wines. I was going to buy floor seats to all the Miami Heat games, because my ultimate goal is to fuck an NBA player right on South Beach. And to top it all off, I was ready for some serious shopping. Even though I was born and raised in the hood, I still wanted the finer things in life.

Just as I was ready to climb on top of Trent, the phone rang. Grandma called to say she was leaving work early so that we could be at the hospital with Oshyn.

"Grandma, I'm good! I'll see her when she gets home!" I yelled. "I'm busy!" I snapped, wanting to get her off the phone.

"I'm sick of jur mouf. That's jur blood, the only one ju got. Ju better be ready when I get there!" And with that she hung up the phone.

I wasn't interested in being by Oshyn's side. I could've honestly cared less whether I went to see her or not. Oshyn always got everything she wanted. She didn't know what struggle was. The spoiled bitch always had it easy, and it just wasn't fair. She wasn't good at everything, because Trent kept crawling back to me.

"Come here, baby," I whined, running my fingers across his moist six-pack.

I gave him another show by fingering my shaved pussy until his dick got hard again. He loved a shaved pussy, telling me it allowed him more to play with.

"Does my pussy taste good?" I asked, sticking my juice dipped French manicured fingers in his mouth. I moaned as his thick tongue wrestled with my fingers. "Tell me how good it tastes!"

Not giving him a chance to answer, I climbed on top of him, kissing him passionately. I grabbed my hard nipples, bending my head down slightly to suck on them. This was his favorite position.

"I'm ready for your dick!" I confessed, trying to stick it in. "Can I have it now?"

"Ooohhhhh!" Trent moaned, as I slid it in. "Your pussy is so wet!"

I rode his dick like a stallion, feeling my ass jiggling out of control. He grabbed my fat ass and slapped it until it stung with pleasure. I liked it rough.

"Fuck me, daddy!" I demanded, biting my lower lip.

"Fuck…me…har..der!"

He flipped me over on my stomach and put his big dick in my pussy from the back. He pumped his rock hard dick into me harder and faster, trying to release all his hurt and guilt into me. I clinched my eyes shut and bit my grandmother's old flat pillow in an attempt to endure the pain that felt so good.

"Chloe?" my grandma asked confused, standing at the door, trying to convince herself that it wasn't me fucking the man that left my pregnant cousin for dead.

I stopped and opened up my eyes. *She wasn't supposed to be here for another hour*, I thought to myself as Trent quickly slid out of me.

"How could ju?" she asked, with a stern voice. When my grandma got upset, her Spanish accent made it almost impossible to understand her. "Ju wicked, wicked child! Just like ju mother. Ju bring this devil into my home and lay with him in my bed? Get out!"

I looked in her old wrinkled eyes, eyes that were once so happy, so full of life. In them I saw my mother. My grandmother, although aged, looked just like her, stunningly beautiful. Her silky, long black hair, which ran in the family, was in one big braid that laid over her shoulder, resting on her visibly sagging left breast.

I didn't say anything and neither did Trent. We couldn't. Trent was already struggling to zip up his pants, as I rushed to gather my things from the floor. I noticed that my grandmother was leaning on her dresser and clenching her heart. I couldn't help but wonder if I was the cause.

"Grandma, you okay?" I asked, reaching out to touch her.

"Get jur filthy hands off of me, ju wicked child!" She immediately busted out in a cold sweat. "I do all I can for ju. Raised ju since ju were eight, and ju still follow in the devil's footsteps."

"My mother is not the devil!" I hollered at her like an adolescent having a temper tantrum. I reacted that way whenever she said those awful things about my mother.

"Oh yes child, jur mother was the devil, and so are ju! I should've given ju away like they told me to, but I refused to give up hope and then ju do this. This is the only family ju have and ju do this to jur only cousin. In my home…oh God!"

"Grandma, what's wrong?" I asked again, this time noticing that Trent had left the house.

Her eyes rolled to the back of her head as she fell to the ground, hitting her head on the dresser. I dialed 911 and asked for help. I checked her pulse and realized she wasn't breathing. I panicked! The operator said the paramedics were on the way, but I wasn't sure that they'd make it in time.

I did something I hadn't done in a while. I prayed, hoping that it wasn't too late.

# 3

# *CHLOE*

## (2007)

I knew money when I saw it, and wealth was written all over his body. The way he threw stacks of money on the crap table told me he was my kind of guy. Italian, French, and possibly Jewish, I didn't have a clue about his nationality, but one thing was for sure, tonight he would be mine.

As usual, my plan was in order. From across the room, my neck stretched so far I thought it was about come out of the socket. I watched him closely as he lost four thousand dollars on one roll and thought nothing of it; his expression never changed. Hell, I loved Atlantic City. I could always count on catching a sugar daddy.

I listened to those who began to crowd around the crap table as they whispered amongst themselves.

"Damn, he's a high roller for sure," one woman said, standing near me.

The man I silently claimed for the night had the

whole table on lock. The reserved sign sitting on the edge of the wooden ledge told all the fake ballers to back the fuck up. I instantly got wet at the thought of him having that kind of power.

He was a handsome man, but nonetheless, white. A bit older, around fifty, his distinguished look was a turn on. I had never been with an older white man before, but hell, their money spent too. At first glance he could've been George Clooney's twin. Then I thought, *nah, more like Taylor Hicks from American Idol.*

I looked around and laughed to myself at the crowd of wannabes and the high priced hoes trying to snatch up a player. Everybody thinks that the hood and high class America are different, but in a sense, we're all the same. At the end of the day, the men want pussy and the women want that paper, regardless of their nationality.

Me and my girl, Joy, decided to move in closer, joining the nosey crowd. Like everyone else, we observed the game, minus the hooping and hollering every time he rolled a good number. My mind stayed focused on the stacks of chips he had in front of him. I wasn't a big time gambler, but I knew black chips meant hundreds, and the pink chips he threw around like it was nothing, was really worth $5,000 a whop.

For some reason, the distinguished stranger looked up and flashed a perfect smile. Fortunately, he was looking at me, and only me. *Definitely porcelain veneers,* I thought to myself, as I smiled back and admired his expensive grill. I returned the gesture with a friendly wave, and flashed my ten-carat diamond bracelet, signaling to him that my time would cost.

While he continued to play, gambling thousands, his mischievous blue eyes stayed glued to me every chance he got. I guess with my skin-tight red Valentino dress showing off my perfect breast and plumped round ass, everyone's eyes stayed glued to me.

Joy looked sexy too, rocking a skin tight strapless blue Gucci dress that looked like it had been painted on. Every now and then I was into bitches and Joy was a bad one, thick in all the right places, plus she knew how to get money. She was half Jamaican and a pure freak, pretty in the face and had a deep pussy like mine.

We both sipped our champagne, discreetly posing for the high priced admirers, when I got a light tap on my shoulder.

"The gentleman, Mr. Bourdeaux, says to enjoy the rest of your stay here," the burly messenger said, pointing to the man that had been eyeing me.

"And who are you?" I asked, wanting to know the affiliation.

He ignored me, handed me two pink chips and said, "Mr. Bourdeaux wants you to cash these in. Start with $10,000, but tonight, skies the limit." I didn't want to act like I was impressed, so I snatched the chips and walked off. "Meet us in the lobby at midnight," he called out, then disappeared.

The stranger, Mr. Bourdeaux, continued to play his game as if nothing happened. I excused myself from Joy, and walked over to introduce myself and thank him for his generosity. Everyone looked at me like I was crazy when I walked up on him.

"Miss, this is a private table, sweetie," one of the pit bosses said, with sarcasm. The wench clearly wanted him to stay and lose all his money.

"I'm with him," I shot back, and gritted on the bitch.

"Are you this kind to all the ladies?" I whispered to him, in my sexiest voice. I brushed against his body softly, teasing him with my tits.

He enjoyed every minute of it, and obviously didn't care who was watching. "Most of the time, but only when they are as beautiful as you."

The white man was honest and I liked that. I spotted the wedding band on his finger. He was married, most of them were. Perfect.

"What do you do?" I asked, curious to know who I was dealing with.

"We will discuss that in due time, my dear."

"Well, thank you again for being so kind," I said, turning around to walk away.

"Wait," he said, grabbing my arm. "What's your name?"

"Chloe."

"Well, Chloe, after you and your lady friend over there indulge in a little shopping spree, I'll have my driver pick you up in front of the hotel at midnight. Please be punctual, I'm a busy man."

I smiled and walked away, ready to spend every dime of the money he'd given me.

❀   ❀   ❀

Twenty thousand dollars is what we spent between the two of us. We spent our new victim's money and some of our own too. I had a very expensive habit that, at this point, needed some TLC. It gave me a high that I knew was temporary, but it put me at a place I needed to be. The top.

Me and Joy stocked up on diamonds, shoes, clothes, and I even picked up a few furs for the winter. I still had no idea what Mr. Bourdeaux did, but whatever it was, he was a powerful man and could afford to pay me back for any extra money I'd spent.

After shopping, we walked to the hotel lobby where Mr. Bourdeaux said to meet him. Right on time, we were greeted by the driver of his crispy, black Maybach Mercedes. His posh driver opened the door and waited patiently while we both climbed in.

"These are for you," the driver said, as he gently placed the soft black velvet boxes in each of our hands.

We opened them, and our eyes lit up as we gazed at the pink diamond earrings he gave us. We wasted no time putting them on and rode in the plush car, trying to silently plot our next move.

Me and Joy had initially plotted to rob the white man after a night full of fun. The pay-off surely would have put us at our target goal for this week. He would've been our fourth victim, and with the other three, we had already racked in a nice ninety thousand dollars. This is what my life had amounted to after I spent my mother's life insurance money. Fifty thousand dollars was all I had left from the half a million I got when I turned twenty-one. Now at twenty-five, I did anything to keep up with the lavish lifestyle I had become accustomed to living.

Many would ask how I could fuck up that much money in so little time. I mean, it takes some people their whole lives to accumulate that kind of paper. Well, for me it was easy!

As soon as my money came in, I bought a four bedroom, three and a half bathroom house for three hundred thousand dollars. Then I splurged and paid cash for my 2003 Escalade truck that I copped for sixty thousand. Not to mention, for the last year, I've been traveling from state-to state, living in lavish hotels, looking for lavish men. A basic home was no longer enough for me.

At twenty-five years old, I had become everything that I'd ever dreamed. Besides, being the talk of everybody's town and the envy of all, put me on top; above everyone else, even Oshyn. I shopped in Tokyo, Milan and Paris. I gambled my money away with the top dogs in Vegas, and became a regular at the five star hotels, presidential suites, of course. I bought out the bar at every upscale nightclub that was home to the ballers, making myself comfortable around the A-listers. I spent well over a thousand dollars daily, and had nothing to show for it, except my banging VVS stone bracelet that I got from Jacob the Jeweler. And just like Kimora Lee Simmons, my wardrobe could style a small country.

As the Maybach floated through the city streets, I had a hunch there was something impressively different about this man. I figured the money would be greater if I were patient, so I tapped Joy on the leg and shook my head no, letting her know that the initial plans we had for the night were off. I could tell from the look on her face she was pissed, but I dared her to buck at me. I was in charge.

When we got to our destination, the driver escorted us up to his boss' hotel suite and excused himself back downstairs. We let ourselves in the twenty-two hundred square foot room, and were greeted by thousands of red long stemmed roses. The room was pitch black, but the flames from candles that belly danced off the walls, allowed for little lighting.

With the room dimly lit, I was able to make out Mr. Bourdeaux's silhouette in the corner sitting in a reclining chair. He was dressed in a black satin robe, velvet Chinese slippers, and he puffed slowly on a Cuban cigar. Instantly, I got Joy's attention and signaled her to follow me into the bathroom. Within moments, we changed our gear, and reported center stage in front of Mr. Bourdeaux.

Me and Joy simultaneously dropped our matching red trench coats to the floor and walked over to him, wearing nothing but our stilettos and the huge pink diamond earrings, compliments of his shopping spree. The room was so quiet, you could hear a pin drop on the carpeted floors.

Joy walked behind the chair, and I positioned myself in front of him, placing both hands on my hips so that he could admire my beauty. He squinted his eyes as he took another puff of his awful smelling cigar and licked his lips. Without warning, I lifted my foot up and played tricks with his dick as hard and erotic as I could. His robe wasn't tied together, which allowed me to see that I had nailed my heel right into his balls. It looked like it was painful, and by the sound of his whimpering, I was right.

"How do you want it?" I whispered to him, slowly placing my designer heels back on the ground.

Before he got a chance to answer me, Joy snatched the belt from his robe and wrapped it around his neck as tightly as she could. He dropped his cigar, struggling to get free. While his face turned beet red, he attempted to break loose.

Coming to his rescue, I got down on my knees and put his little pink dick in my mouth. I sucked it as hard as I could, stopping right before he came. Joy let go of her death grip and removed her weapon of pleasure as he attempted to regain his composure, caressing his bruised neck. Joy got down on her knees and licked my pussy. My loud, sensuous moaning caught his attention, and for the rest of the night, we all indulged in painful pleasures.

The night ended enjoyably for us all. Before it was all said and done, I was hit with another $10,000 and Joy was hit off with a small stack too. We made plans to see each other every weekend for the next month, giving me a chance to potentially make an estimated forty thousand dollars.

As the weeks passed, the money was great, and despite the fact that he actually had a wife, he treated me far better than her. He seemed to worship the ground I walked on and I wouldn't have it any other way. Months later though, things started to change. His time allotted for me began to decrease, and the vacations that had become common were slim. I knew that if I didn't act fast, I would lose everything I had gained so far, and I couldn't let that happen.

After a few days of not speaking to him, I knew that it was time to go ahead with my alternate plan. Through a reliable source and a lot of money, I had gotten Bourdeaux's home number. I had already sent him a surprise, so I knew he'd be expecting my phone call.

I grinned a wicked smile as I grabbed the phone to make my call. I blocked the number, hoping he would still answer.

"Hello, my little white freakazoid." I laughed, hysterically into the receiver.

"What do you want from me?" he asked, with a hint of fear in his voice.

I laughed once again, before repeating his comment. "What do I want from you? Everything you got!" I said, in a more serious tone.

"Why would you do this to me after everything I've done for you? I flew you around the world in my private jet, and took you to extravagant events that my wife didn't even go to."

*Spare me*, I thought. I was losing respect for his ass the more he talked. Here he was sitting on the phone whining like a lil' punk, and had millions stashed all around the world.

"I kept you in the finest handmade Italian gowns, made sure you wanted for nothing, and this is how you show your gratitude?" he shouted.

He was referring to the picture I had e-mailed him in a doggy style position with me shoving a dildo up his ass.

"Why Chloe?" he asked, with desperation in his voice.

"Baby, it's all business, nothing personal." I had Mr. Bourdeaux right where I wanted him, eating out the palm of my hands.

"How much do you want for the picture, Chloe?" he said, calming down a bit. I didn't have to see him to know he was probably sweating like a pig. He continued, trying to figure out what his ransom was going to be. "How much?" he asked, totally out of his element. Being in control was all he'd ever known, and to have his life threatened by a black woman was pure torture to him. I loved every moment of it! "I'll give you two hundred thousand dollars," he finally blurted out.

"Two hundred thousand? Are you trying to play me? That won't even last me a week! You are *THE* Shannon Bourdeaux, CEO of one of the wealthiest investment banking firms in France. You're worth millions, and you dare insult my intelligence by offering me not even five percent of what you're worth? Maybe you didn't realize what I sent you SO LET ME BREAK IT DOWN! I sent you a picture of your prominent hairy ass on all fours with a blonde wig on and some lacy red lingerie. Now that's pretty bad for a man of your stature. But to make matters worse, you have *yours truly* sticking a plastic dick in your ass!"

"Oh, Chloe, don't do this!"

"Why not?" I joked. "You were loving it so much, your dumb ass didn't even notice Joy taking the pictures." I paused to see if he was still on the line. He hadn't said a word, but I heard his off beat breathing on the other end. "Besides, if your wife finds out and divorces you, she'll get half! So, I think that one million dollars will suffice for me." Although there was complete silence on the other end of the line, I continued with my game plan. "The money needs to be in unmarked one hundred dollar bills, and delivered to my hotel room by noon. If I wake up and there's no money for me…well you figure out what'll happen."

"Are you still staying in New York?" he asked.

"For now," I smirked. He knew I switched residences like I changed my panties. My rich lover hung up the phone, probably relieved that a million would fix everything. He just wanted me and those pictures out of his life, and by paying me off, was a sure way of doing it.

❀    ❀    ❀

I woke up the next day, after hearing a knock on the door. I sprinted like Jackie Joyner Kerse, the Olympic runner. On the ground laid several black duffle bags. I wanted to say thank you to the tall figure walking away from my door, but it seemed like he had absolutely no words for me. I smiled at the delivery and the thought of being a million dollars richer. Pimping was definitely not easy.

Since Mr. Bourdeaux was a made man, I knew he had a lot of power. Enough power to soon have me killed and never found. I knew that he would never feel safe knowing I had the other copy of that picture, and he was right.

I had made the decision to keep moving around for a few months instead of settling down in one spot, maybe even check out my lame-ass cousin down south. At least there I would be a fresh face and no one would be looking for me. As an adult, I never had a job and wouldn't be able to spend all this paper without the FEDs getting involved. I needed to be able to account for this amount of paper, so I concluded that I would lay low for a while and clean up my money.

I called Joy to let her know that the deal went through and let her in on the new plan. She agreed to stay in New York for a while to handle a few things, and would hook up with me soon.

# 4

# OSHYN

## (2007)

Church. It had been a while since I'd been, but my grandma insisted that I show up. I moved her to Raleigh, NC with me last year, and she had already found a good church home. It was the type of church where the female pillars of the community showed up in large brim hats, waiting to hear the latest gossip after church.

To my surprise, Grandma fit right in. She smiled headed down the aisle, waving to every person in the sanctuary, looking better than the preacher's wife. We took our seats in front of the sanctuary, which is where she said God preferred us to sit.

My cousin, Chloe, dressed for the Oscars in her twenty-two hundred dollar St. John suit sat to the left of Grandma, exhausted from the night before. She showed up at my house in the wee hours of the morning, after hoeing all night. Chloe always had long nights.

Supposedly, she was here to spend a little time with

me and Grandma, but it seemed her time was focused on meeting every paid dude in the city of Raleigh. I passed Chloe a note, telling her that she wasn't at a fashion show. She read it, gave me her middle finger, tilted her hat back down, and dozed off.

My best friend, Apples and her daughter, Bella, got comfortable next to me and my son, Micah, who was getting restless on the barely cushioned seats. I was relieved to see that Apples took up my grandmother's invitation to come to church. She had just moved to North Carolina a couple of months ago, and was trying to create a new life for her and Bella, a life that her psycho baby father tried to steal.

The choir got up for praise and worship and I sang along, while peeping over at Chloe, who resembled a dead log. *Lord, please forgive her*, I prayed, hoping He'd look beyond her faults. She was a bad apple, rotten to the core, but she was still family. I took my mind off of Chloe and focused on the service.

The church was beautiful. A giant crystal chandelier hung from the arched ceilings and beautifully scripted bible quotes graced the walls. The atmosphere was warm, and I definitely felt safe.

We rose as the preacher got up to speak. Bishop Tim Nedo was a prophetic speaker, who had the anointing of God over his life. I smiled inside at the thought of being in church, and hoped Chloe was feeling good too. After all, we were raised in church. Pentecostal in fact, whatever that meant, and our grandmother made sure we attended every service growing up.

I was as attentive as I could be in the message entitled, *Knowing Who You Are Through God,* when a man sitting off to the side caught my eye. His dark, chiseled skin seemed to slightly glow, making him look like an angel from heaven. I could tell his body was made of brick through his tailor made gray suit. He was clean-cut and handsome.

This mystery man held my attention until his eyes caught mine drooling all over him. I snapped back into reality, hoping my stare wasn't obvious and focused back on the pulpit. Eventually church had come to an end, and I was ready to get out of my Yves Saint Lauren suit and go shopping.

I made my way to the outside of the church, hoping to get a glimpse of the fine man I had stared down like a suspect. But he was nowhere to be found. The temperature outside had already reached 90 degrees and was climbing. August was like that down south.

After church, I threw on a wife beater, jean skirt, and Fendi flip-flops. Chloe, always trying to draw attention to herself, had on a pair of booty shorts, a Gucci tank top and some Jimmy Choo stilettos.

We both had appointments to get our pedicures done, and I had an appointment for a bootleg dubi wrap. *No one does the shit like the Dominicans back home,* I thought. I remembered trying to explain the style to my under-trained stylist. It was supposed to be blown out, not wrapped around.

Within minutes, Chloe and I jumped in my new silver 645i BMW, made it the mall, and I headed straight to the salon. We agreed to meet at the food court once our day of beauty and light shopping were complete.

Before I knew it, I was in the chair being set up once again. No matter what I said, the girl just couldn't get it right. Thank God for my good grain of hair. I tipped the non-styling wench and walked out with an attitude, while trying to tame the wild strands, only to give up. I should have left this shit in a ponytail.

I shopped a little bit, picking up a fly hat for Grandma, but nothing major. My eyes bulged out my head when I spotted Chloe. She had bags galore hanging off her shoulder, and draped over her arms.

"What's all of this?" I asked.

"Here, I need help," she answered, and shot me a dirty look.

"I have to stop at the bookstore on the way out," I told her, while grabbing a few of the bags.

"Hell no! Don't nobody wanna be in the fucking bookstore with you all day," she said, raising her tone. "That shit is too educational. All your lonely ass do all day is read them dumb ass books. Get a fucking life and take me home!" Chloe demanded.

"Shut the fuck up before I make you walk home. You must have forgot I drove," I reminded her, dangling the car keys in her face as I walked ahead, rolling my eyes.

"Walk home? If I wanted to, I'd have a helicopter come and get me right now! Walk home...I don't know who the fuck you think you talking to."

"I'm talking to you, broke bitch! You could've had a helicopter come and get you if you had given me your bread to invest, but Noooo, your stupid ass spent it all. So like I said, shut the fuck up before I make you walk home!"

"I dare you," Chloe said, wanting me to challenge her.

"Dare me? I left your ass before and I'll do it again, keep talking," I said, reminding her of when I left her at the grocery store because of her slick mouth.

Chloe hadn't even been in Raleigh a month, and already we were going at each other's throat. I hated it when she took me out of my character. I was trying to get my life together, maintaining my position as a businesswoman as much as possible, and she reminded me of where I ran from, the hood.

We were not that close and often disagreed, but we always seemed to be together. Being raised by our grandmother, we had no choice.

At twenty-five, she was still drop dead gorgeous, standing at five seven and one hundred and forty-nine pounds. Her body was like raw meat to a starving tiger; wherever she went the men followed. It seemed to run in the family. Her golden brown complexion told everyone of the Puerto Rican blood that ran through our veins. We were both mixed, but Chloe looked like she came straight off the boat. Her eyes were slanted, making you think she was of Asian decent. She may have been since no one, including her mom, knew who her daddy was. Her jet black hair went to the middle of her back. She kept it in soft curls most of the time, leaving it looking flawless wherever she went. Chloe's beauty was echoed by that of her belated mother, Mahogany, and unfortunately, so was her personality.

She was a year older than me, and like Chloe and I, my mother, Rosalyn and Aunt Mahogany, were also two completely different people. They both grew up dirt poor and were raised by their mother, Rose Rodriguez. The thought of my grandmother made me smile, but the familiar man standing in front of the bookstore clouded my vision.

He stood six five and had to be about two hundred and fifty pounds. He had skin that reminded me of a Hershey's kiss and sported a low cut ceaser with deep waves. His light gray eyes pierced my body as he stared at me with the determination of a pit bull. He smiled at me, showing off his perfect white teeth with a slight gap in the middle. He wore a black tee, a pair of Replay jeans and black Gucci sneakers. He was fly, but I wasn't impressed. You can always be fly and broke, and I hated that type.

I positioned myself to where he could see me, never

being too noticeable. Our eyes met again, he smiled. I returned the gesture and walked away.

He followed.

No matter how much they wanted to deny it, men loved the art of chase if done right…and I was good at it.

"Girl, he's fine as hell!" Chloe pointed out to me, showing no discretion at all. I rolled my eyes at her lack of dignity.

"He's alright," I said, hating that she was with me.

"Pardon me, Ma. My name is Brooklyn. I saw you in church today. What's your name?" he asked, extending his hand.

"Here you go," I said, shaking my head. "Everybody wants to be from New York. Raleigh is a pretty cool place, it's okay to claim it." I was so sick of everyone down south pretending they were from up top. It was something that really got on my nerves.

"Ma, I don't have to lie and I never caught your name," he said smoothly, ignoring my sarcasm and taking it upon himself to place my hand in his.

*Um! He's definitely a leader*, I thought, recalling all the other guys I intimidated. At twenty-four, I made a lot of money, and looked like I made paper too. Most guys couldn't handle that, but he seemed to have potential.

"Your name?" he asked again.

"Oshyn," I said as I smiled, showing off the deep dimples my dad gave me. It was the only thing he'd ever given me.

I stared at the man I admired at church today. He looked even better up close than he did pews away.

"It's a pleasure," he said, kissing the back of my hand. I eased away from his grasp and entered the store.

I caught a glimpse of Chloe out the side of my eye pouting because he wasn't paying her any attention. She was always so extra, over the top, and me so simple. Maybe that's what he wanted, a little simplicity.

"Real estate, huh?" he wondered, looking at the book in my hand.

"Yeah, I just started my own company." I was hesitant. I hated revealing things to strangers.

"Can we go now?" Chloe chimed in.

I ignored her and went into a daze thinking about how Trent instilled in me not to trust anyone. Here it was years later, and I was still living like a hustler's wife. To this day, only immediate family could come to my house. I still watched for police and helicopters in my rear view mirror to see if they were following me, and I watched what was said over the phone. This was a habit that was hard to break.

"That's a good business. Lots of money in that," Brooklyn said, trying to keep the conversation going.

"What?" I asked aggravated, as I snapped out of my own little world. All I heard was money, and that wasn't something I felt like he should have been talking about.

"Real estate, remember?" he said, talking to me like I

was a slow child. "You said that you just started your own company, and I said that there was a lot of money in it."

"Oh, yeah, it sure is," I said embarrassed. I flashed him a closed lip smile.

"You have dimples."

"Sometimes."

"They're beautiful," he said.

I changed the subject, because I never took compliments well. "Looks like you bought the whole store," I said, noticing the five Louie Vuitton bags at his feet.

"It's my mom's birthday and she loves designer bags."

"That's sweet of you," I said, with a hint of sarcasm. I didn't trust men. No matter how sweet one portrayed to be, they all weren't shit in my book.

I looked down at Chloe as she picked up a pile of books off the floor. *Oh, now the bitch wants to read,* I thought, as she tried her best to get Brooklyn's attention with her ass all in his face. I turned around and walked away towards the check out counter. I didn't feel like dealing with her issues right now.

"That'll be forty-two dollars and twenty-six cents," the old woman said to me, as she bagged my books.

"Miss, I'll take care of the ladies order," Brooklyn said, making his presence known.

I guess this was his way of letting me know that he was interested in me, and not Chloe. It shocked me because most men liked thick, video-type chicks, while I was barely a size six. Over the years, my weight increased, but I was still struggling to hit 110 pounds.

Before I knew it, Brooklyn took out a crispy one hundred dollar bill, and placed it on the counter. "There's more where that came from. Consider it sowing a seed into your future," he said, directing his comment back to me.

I rolled my eyes and handed a fifty-dollar bill to the old woman behind the counter. I was wise enough to know that gifts were never free and came with a price.

"That doesn't impress me," I said, shaking my head. "Why don't you go holla at her, I know she'll take it," I said, referring to my cousin, who was now pacing back and forth.

"I'm sorry if I offended you. I'm just glad to see a sister doing something for herself, and I wanted to help out."

"Help out? I don't need your charity. I live very well," I snapped.

"Listen, I have to go, but I would love to make all of this up to you by taking you to dinner tonight." He waited anxiously for an answer, while I gave him the, 'I might be busy look.' "Ma, I'm not going anywhere until you say yes," he said, putting his bags down and crossing his arms.

I ignored his determination, assuming he probably did this with all the girls. Hesitantly, I gave him my number and told him to call me. He grabbed my hand, kissing the back of it for the second time, and promised that I'd hear from him by eight. Looking up, he said goodbye to Chloe and walked out the store. I was surprised he knew she was still there. So was she.

As I got ready to leave, I was distracted by a girl that bumped into me, making all my bags drop to the ground. I lost my balance and landed on the floor.

"Watch where the fuck you're going, dumb bitch!" I screamed at her angrily, as I struggled to get back up.

On a normal day, I would have never been that rude, but my intuition was telling me that this was intentional. I looked at the bitch and her five homegirls and didn't remember them from anywhere. She was a cute girl, with a full head of freshly done micro-braids. I tried to gain my composure because I didn't want the old Oshyn to resurface. My Rochester hood days were over.

She walked closer to me, with her flunkies quick on her heels and asked, "Is there a problem?"

"Not if you don't want one," Chloe said, coming to my defense.

No matter how much we argued, she always had my back when it came to a fight. That was at least one family code we stuck to. By now, we had drawn a sizeable crowd and everyone was anxious to see what was going to happen.

"Your girl over here needs to watch where she's going," she said, still calm as if she was right.

I still hadn't said a word, because I wasn't quite sure where she was coming from.

"Aren't you going to say sorry?" she asked, with her hands on her hips.

"Suck my pussy, stupid bitch," Chloe said to her. Her blade was already in the palm of her hands, not visible to the bystanders, but ready to poke her. I had drawn mine too, which made this, another bad habit I couldn't break.

As the commotion continued, I was caught off guard when the bitch spit at me, her nasty saliva landing in my face at full force. Before I could even blink, Chloe lunged in ready to slice, when two officers came our way to see what was going on. It was only by the grace of God that they came when they did, because Chloe was about to kill that girl. Spitting in somebody's face is the ultimate disrespect, and I was going to make sure she paid.

As the unknown girls walked away, the broad who bumped me turned around to leave me with a devilish wink. I didn't know who she was, but I promised her through my eyes, that I would find her one day. It is, after all, a small world.

# 5

# OSHYN

We left the mall shortly after the altercation and headed to my house.

"I can't believe you let that bitch spit in your face," Chloe said, smiling as she reclined the passenger seat back.

"What the fuck did you want me to do, go to jail? I don't live on the edge like you. I have a business to run," I said, making it clear that she didn't. "I'm responsible now, unlike yourself. So, fuck you," I said, turning the radio up. I was not in the mood to go back and forth with her. At least not right now.

"No, she fucked you!" Chloe said, pointing at my tainted face. She turned the music back down and let out a laugh that sent chills up my spine. She was obviously happy that this happened. "Let me find out you moved to North Carolina and got soft. The Oshyn I know would've cut that bitch into pieces and…"

"CHLOE!" I screamed loudly. "I'm not in the fucking mood, shut up," I demanded.

"Don't get all tough now," she said, taunting my sudden urge to fight. She laughed for a few more seconds to herself and then remained quiet for the rest of the ride. Fifteen minutes later, we pulled up at my crib.

I owned a French country designed home, with four beautifully designed bedrooms and three spacious bathrooms. It featured a home theater, and my favorite room in the house, the library. In such a short time, I had done exceptionally well for myself, and would give anything for Trent to see me now.

I remember the day I got out the hospital. I went back to the house we once called home, and dug up the twelve g's taken from his stash. Trent wouldn't allow me to work and had stopped giving me bread when I asked for it, so looking out for myself was crucial. I guess I was saving it for emergencies like this. Call it women's intuition, but the end was clear and unavoidable. I caught the Greyhound bus to Raleigh the same night with my newborn baby and stayed in a hotel until I found an apartment, which only took me about a week.

I had never been to North Carolina before, but Raleigh seemed like a nice place to be. I thought they had palm trees though, and didn't know it snowed. Guess I thought I was moving to the Bahamas.

I chose not to go to college when I got here, realizing that it was me against the world. I couldn't see myself thirty thousand dollars in debt and paying back loans. It was a burden I didn't want to put on myself. I wanted to start my own multi-million dollar corporation, and was determined to have it. I figured it couldn't be that hard. People like Oprah and Bill Gates showed me that it was possible to make it to the top, because of their vision and determination. I too had a vision and a whole lot of faith that was going to take my real estate company to the top.

A homeless man once told me that necessity and fear were the best motivators. I knew the lifestyle I wanted to live, and I needed to make major changes and take big risks to make it happen.

Chloe and I walked into the house, throwing the bags across the couch. Despite all the drama that had happened today, I was still in a decent mood.

"Apples, I'm here!" I yelled to my best friend. She had agreed to watch Micah for me while Chloe and I went to the mall.

"What did you get me?" Apples asked, walking over to the shopping bags.

"Some spit," Chloe answered, while she poured herself some juice.

"What?" Apples said, more aggravated that Chloe had butted in on her conversation than anything else.

"Some bitch at the mall spit in my face."

"What!" Apples said again. She crossed her arms, waiting for all the details.

"It was nothing. The police came before I could get

her and…I really don't want to talk about this right now."

"Who was she? Did you know her?" she asked, not ready to drop the subject.

"No, I've never seen her before."

Chloe walked away, still laughing to herself at the show she had witnessed. She grabbed her cell phone and headed toward the deck.

"I got my god daughter two pairs of Prada ballerina shoes." I dangled the shoes in the air, trying to change the subject. Bella was only six years old and such a prima dona.

Just then, Bella entered the room. "These are hot Auntie, thanks!" she said, grabbing them to try them on.

"You're welcome princess."

I watched as Apples drop down to the floor to help Bella try them on. It was nice to see her happy and interacting with her child.

"They fit," Bella called out.

"Thanks so much, Oshyn," Apples said, showing her appreciation.

"Anything for you," I said.

Apples, born Charlene Davis, was my best friend. Although originally from The Big Apple, her sparkling green eyes is where she got the name. When I first met her, I remembered being amazed at seeing a black girl with green eyes. She told me that her dad was white and her mother, black, which explained her light skin and spontaneous freckles that adorned her nose. She was absolutely gorgeous and stood about five eleven, weighing one hundred and thirty-five pounds. She reminded you of a runway model. No boobs, B cup...maybe.

Her hair, once full of long tight ringlets, was now shoulder length, brown with blonde highlights, and she kept it straightened. Her look made you think she was from the islands, and shocked you when she said she was from the hood. She was very well spoken and usually enunciated each word.

I met her in Rochester almost ten years ago. Apples was one of the flyest bitches I knew. Carrying books to school in Gucci backpacks in the eighth grade was unheard of. All the bitches hated, and she was welcomed to school everyday with a fight. Despite how attractive she was, the kids led by an eighth grader named Stacey, nicknamed Apples the green-eyed monster. Stacey felt that her position, as the most popular girl at Jefferson Middle School, was being threatened by the new chick from the city, and she was right. Everyone, especially the niggas, flocked to Apples and she even had the high school boys picking her up after class in their Lexus and Benz's.

Apple's tried hard to avoid any confrontation, until one day Stacey's mouth became intolerable. Apples definitely held it down, and no other bitch tested her when Stacey was rushed to the hospital with her neck ripped open. Thank God she lived. Real recognized real, and I knew we'd get along just fine. At fourteen, she was forced to live with her grandma after her mother killed her boyfriend, and then committed suicide.

Apples told me that her mother had come home early from work one day. In the house, on her bed, she caught her boyfriend with another man's dick shoved up his ass. She said that her mother went crazy and tried to kill both the faggots that ruined her life. Shortly after that, her mother took a test that positively revealed full blown AIDS. Apples said that her mother talked to her about the deadly condition and the possible outcome.

The next day, surprisingly, Apples came home and found her mother and the boyfriend's body in a pool of blood. She said that when she closes her eyes at night, she still sees the pieces of brain that were splattered all over her living room. Apples doesn't talk about it much. Guess I wouldn't either.

I moved Apples and Bella from Rochester to North Carolina into one of the town homes I own about six months ago. She was in a relationship beyond abusive and couldn't get out. That was something I never understood about Apples. After all she had seen me go through with Trent, I never expected her to follow in my footsteps. She was without a doubt one of the strongest women I'd ever met, yet she was so weak. Apples met her ex-boyfriend, Quon, when she was fifteen, and he was twenty-five.

Quon was a don, getting money and had made a name for himself in Rochester as 'The Hitman.' He was known for his ruthless killing style—leaving his victims duct taped and ass-naked. People from all over paid him big time when they wanted a job done, which meant, anything Apple's wanted she could have. It's been said that he's also responsible for a sixty million dollar drug empire that he organized in 1997. Nonetheless, they fucked a few times and fell in love.

She purposely got pregnant to make her lavish lifestyle more permanent…and permanent it had become. Quon was a wild and reckless dude, and word on the streets was that he had a body count in the twenties. Maybe that's where his anger came from, the curse of taking a life. With the devil creating a war in his mind, he was constantly stressed and he took it out on Apples. He'd become obsessed with her and extremely jealous. He would beat the shit out of Apples if another man even looked at her.

She tried hard, but couldn't hide anything from me. Her light skin and bad lies told me everything. Time and time again I pleaded with her to leave him, and although she would agree, the six hundred thousand dollar home in Pittsford, New York was an offer too big to refuse, even if it did feel like a prison. He bought her that when she was nineteen as an apology for sending her to the hospital with a broken collarbone. I had begged her to move down south, but fear had consumed her mind, body and soul.

The last straw came when he beat her ass and Bella ran in to help her mother. He hit the baby so hard she lost two teeth. When he left the house, Apples called me and begged for help. I sent her to Western Union, told her not to pack a thing, and to be on the next flight to North Carolina.

We took pictures of the bruises, and got a restraining order against Quon. Apples even decided to press charges. The police never found him. Didn't really expect them too either. What good are they anyway?

Micah and Bella shot pass me, making enough noise to bring me out of my trance.

"Are you spending the night again?" I asked Apples, realizing she hadn't packed her bags.

"Yeah, I promised Bella and Micah popcorn and a movie."

I didn't mind. A playmate for Micah wasn't that bad, and you could hardly tell they were there. Apples was very clean, quiet, and respected space, unlike Chloe's ass.

"What are you up to tonight?" Apples asked.

"Well, I may step out again. I have a date."

"Finally! Thank God!"

"What is that suppose to mean?" I said, offended.

"When is the last time you've been with a man?" Apples asked, with her hands on her hips.

"Mind your business," I shot back, rolling my eyes.

"Trent really fucked you up, huh?"

I shrugged my shoulders, while the water welled up in my eyes. It had been six years, and I still couldn't let go of the past and forgive. The only man I had ever loved, ever known, had left my son and I for dead.

Since that day, my focus has been on getting money and nothing else. I put money before love, and had set a goal to own so much real estate that I would never have to work again. Being a mother took most of my time, and I rarely made room for anything else. My goal was to be set financially in five to ten years.

"All I'm saying is that you work too much! You need to start enjoying yourself. Who knows, you may even find a husband," Apples said, walking into the kitchen.

"Whatever!" I said, walking away.

I put my phone on the charger and hopped in the shower. The steam from the hot water felt good running down my back. I was relaxed, enjoying myself for about five minutes, when the phone rang.

I rushed out the shower, with my cream satin robe clinging to my wet body, trying to get the phone before it stopped ringing.

"Who is this?" I asked rudely, wondering who was calling from a blocked number.

"Hey, this is Brooklyn. May I speak to Oshyn?" he asked, knowing it was me.

"This is she. What's going on?" I asked flatly.

"Are we still on for our date?"

"I never said I was doing anything, or going

anywhere with you," I snapped back, secretly anxious to go.

"Oh, don't act like that. I just want to take you out and have fun, that's all."

"Yeah, alright," I said, giving in. "Where do you want to meet?"

"What are you in the mood for?"

"Steak."

"Me too."

"How about *J.Kiss*?" I suggested. It was one of the hottest, most expensive steakhouses in Raleigh.

"You have great taste. I like that! Would you like for me to pick you up?"

"Nah, I'm good," I said, not intending to show him where I lived. I still couldn't seem to break those bad habits. "I'll meet you."

"You're a trip! How is nine o'clock?"

"That's fine."

I threw the phone down and sat on the edge of my over-sized king bed. My palms were a bit damp and my heart raced unusually fast. I was a little nervous and scared, all at the same time. I could tell that Brooklyn was different.

He caught my eye the moment I noticed him, and when we first touched, my body started tingling. It was funny, but after we hung up, the tingling returned. I hadn't felt this way about a man in a long time, and he managed to get me wet. I wondered what his hard body would feel like on top of mine. I wondered how soft and passionate his kisses would be all over my body.

My robe fell open, letting my swollen nipples peek out from underneath. It had been a long time since I touched myself and my body was yearning for some attention. I stretched out on my bed and brushed my fingertips against my skin, waking up my senses. I reached over and grabbed my vibrator and dildo out my nightstand. I turned on my vibrator and touched it all over my body. My goose bumps rose at the thought of Brooklyn inside of me. I parted my legs slightly, letting the vibrator gently touch my clit. I grabbed the cyber skin dildo that was beside me and put the head of it into my pussy. I slowly worked the life-like dick in and out of my pleasure garden, while teasing my clit with the vibrator.

"Ummmm," I moaned, as my pussy throbbed, crying for more. I stuck it in harder and faster, moving my hips to the rhythm and pretending that it was Brooklyn's hard dick that I was enjoying. I moaned even louder because the feeling was so intense. I held the vibrator on my clit and pushed the dildo in as fast as I could until my juices gushed out of me.

"Aaaahhhhh!" I screamed. This was the best orgasm that I'd had in a while. I collapsed on my bed and just laid there, panting.

There was a slight knock on the door. "Oshyn, are you okay?" Apples asked, concerned about all the screaming.

"I'm okay," I said, trying to catch my breath. "Just saw a spider, that's all."

# 6

# OSHYN

I pulled up at *J.Kiss* at nine o'clock sharp. My biggest pet peeve was tardiness. I was never late. I reached for my phone to call Brooklyn when I remembered that he had called me from a private number. I released my car to the valet and decided to go in anyway, praying that he was on time. I'd hate to let him go if he wasn't.

I walked into the restaurant and was ambushed by the stale scent of cigar smoke. My long jet black hair was parted down the middle, and rested in the middle of my back. I wanted to look sexy, so I wore my deep red Dolce and Gabbana button up shirt and black satin pencil skirt. My stilettos, which were the classic black Manolo's, were six inches tall, making my legs look like a million dollars. For a petite woman, I was very shapely.

The bar area was flooded with business executives and CEO's, mostly white. As I walked into the room, all the men stared at me with lustful eyes. I always thought that white men fantasized about being with black women. Their long stares only validated my thoughts.

"Oshyn?" I heard a woman's voice say. I turned around, noticing the hostess, and was curious as to how she knew my name.

"Your date will be here shortly," she said, handing me a long stem red rose.

The rose softened me.

A simple rose.

I smiled and helped myself to the bar, ordering a glass of wine. As it arrived, the bartender handed me another rose.

"What's this?"

"Just have fun!" the older man said, giving me a reassuring wink.

"This boy is really trying to turn on the charm," I said to him.

After ordering another glass of wine, I gazed at my diamond Cartier watch and realized that Brooklyn was fifteen minutes late. Although I was starting to get upset, I decided not to make it an issue.

*At least he was thoughtful enough to give me flowers,* I thought to myself. I sat at the bar for another five minutes, sipping on my third drink when I got a light tap on my shoulder. I spun around and was greeted by a dozen red roses.

"I'm so happy you made it!" Brooklyn said, kissing my cheek.

I secretly was too.

"Didn't your mother teach you not to keep a woman waiting?" I asked.

"I'm sorry, Ma. I had to take care of some last minute business. I promise it'll never happen again," Brooklyn said, trying to give me a sad look.

"For your sake, I hope not. I would hate to dismiss you this early in the game," I said, finally excepting the roses.

He laughed at my comment, displaying his beautiful smile.

I immediately turned away. I didn't want him to see me blushing, and besides, that familiar tingling sensation was starting to come back.

Luckily the hostess interrupted the uncomfortable situation by telling us our table was ready. Brooklyn had arranged for a secluded section in the back of the restaurant that was adorned with more red roses.

"Wow, this is beautiful." I said, reaching for my chair.

"Wait! Let me get that for you," Brooklyn said, pulling the chair out for me.

It had been a while since I let a man play his position, and allowed him to treat me like a woman. I was so accustomed to pulling out my own chair and opening up my own door, that I was pleased to know that chivalry wasn't dead.

"You're gorgeous," he said, with a straight face.

"Thank you."

"Your hair is so long," he said, trying to figure out if it was real. "Are you mixed?"

"Yes, my mother is half Puerto Rican, and my father is black."

"That's what's up. Is Oshyn your real name?"

"Yeah," I said, wishing I had a penny for every time someone asked me that.

"Now I've heard of a lot of crazy names, but never Oshyn. Why did your mom name you that?"

"My mother was on a cruise to the Bahamas when she went into labor. They delivered me on the boat and rushed us to the hospital by way of helicopter."

"Wow!" he said amazed.

"She named me Oshyn because that's where I was born. It's much better than her first choice…Carnival," I said, rolling my eyes at the thought of being named after a boat.

Laughing at my sarcasm he said, "That's crazy."

"Yeah, it was crazy to her too because I was supposed to be born in September."

"Oh, so when is your birthday?"

"July the fourth," I stated proudly. I was sure that the Fourth of July was the best birthday to have.

"When is your birthday?"

"June twentieth."

"Cancer?"

"Don't know. I don't believe in signs."

"Me either," I said, wondering why I had even asked.

We both shared a laugh.

"What's your real name?"

"My real name is Brooklyn. Brooklyn Jones. My mother was thirteen when she had me, and was a poster girl for Brooklyn, New York. She loved it, swore by it, and would, even today, die for it, so it was only right that she named me after her stomping grounds. She had my name ready whether I was a boy or a girl. I was born and raised there, and just moved to Raleigh less than a year ago. I tried bringing her with me…but she's Brooklyn for life. I love it here though. It's quiet, calm and warm."

I smiled and silently agreed.

"You're not from here," he told me. "You're too fly, your swagger, your…"

"I'm from upstate New York," I said, cutting him off from all the compliments. I hated blushing and had done enough of it for the night.

"Word? Up top in the building! What part?"

"Rochester," I said confidently.

"That ain't New York, that's Canada," he said, laughing hysterically. I didn't crack a smile, didn't really think it was funny.

"Oh yeah, well come to the Roc and say that shit! Don't sleep!" I was serious, and it was written all over my face.

One thing about us Rochestrians was that we definitely didn't play any games when it came down to where we were from. I laughed inside, thinking about the name I'd just made up.

"But on a serious note, a lot of people found that out the hard way and never left breathing."

"I'm just joking with you," Brooklyn said, sensing the animosity building. "I don't want no beef," he said, with his hands up in surrender position. "I know someone else from Rochester, and they act the same way when I say something about it. All y'all are crazy. It must be something in the water!" he added, still cracking himself up.

"You go to the bookstore often?" I asked, avoiding the talk about Rochester. It was a touchy subject that I'd much rather let go.

"Nah, I saw a beautiful young lady walking that way, and decide to follow my prey."

I smiled, knowing that he was talking about me. I didn't know I still had it. Maybe I had been out the game too long?

"Talk about destiny, I'm so glad we met," he said, kissing the back of my hand.

"Whatever," I said, not interested in his theory about fate. Slowly, I moved my hand away from his tight grasp.

"Do you go to the bookstore often?" Brooklyn asked.

"Almost everyday, I love it. If there were one place I could live in the whole entire world, that's where it would be. The sight of all those books just…" I paused, daydreaming about all the books I wanted.

"You really love books?" he said, trying to figure out

if I had a slight obsession.

"Yeah," I said embarrassed. "A lot."

The waitress showed up with the bottle of Veuve Clicquot champagne Brooklyn had ordered. I didn't drink too often, but it was clear that the bubbly he'd chosen had a big price tag.

"Let's toast to us," he said, raising his glass just as the waitress finished taking our order.

"Aren't you moving a little too fast?" I asked.

"That's how I move, fast. But for now, we'll go at your pace. So, you just started a real estate business?" he asked, lowering his glass.

"Yeah, I like money and don't want to work that hard, so it seemed like the best choice."

"You don't have to work hard?" he asked, with a confused expression.

"Not really. I got a great jump-start in this business. Soon after I got my realtor's license, two of my homeboys that played college ball got drafted into the league and needed a new home. Luckily for me, both of their homes were a million dollars, earning me a sizeable commission."

"That's what's up! I own some real estate in Harlem and hope to buy some property down here. Maybe you could help me?"

"You got bread? I got help."

He laughed. I was serious.

"You're beautiful and smart. How old are you, if you

don't mind me asking?" Brooklyn seemed to admire me way too much. I could tell by the way he looked at me.

"Twenty-four, and you?"

"Twenty-six."

We paused. He stared.

"You're young, very attractive, have so much going for yourself...why are you single?"

"Because I want to be," I said, with force.

"Why?" he asked, not intimidated by my aggression.

"I need to be," I answered, a bit less defensive this time.

"Who did it?" Brooklyn questioned.

"My baby father."

"You have kids?" he asked shocked, while he adjusted himself in the chair.

"I have a son, and he's six."

"Wow! I can't believe that you're a mom."

"Got a problem?" I asked defensively.

"No. I think that's beautiful."

"Do you have any kids?"

"No, not yet."

"That's rare."

"I don't want a baby mother," he said, leaning in closer to me. "I want a wife."

We paused. I stared.

For a minute, I thought I was falling for this handsome dude. I wasn't sure if it was the champagne making me hot, or if he had slipped me a 'Mickey'. I could feel his sweet breath on my face, making my goose bumps rise. My trembling hand reached for the water and tipped it off the table, shattering the glass on the floor. I jumped out the way in time before any of it got on me. The waiter at the next table wasn't so lucky. I apologized for my clumsiness, and while they cleaned up, we returned back to the conversation.

"What line of work are you in?" I asked, uncomfortable about the way he made me sweat.

"When?"

"When you're not beating off," I said seriously. He laughed at my humor, not expecting that reply.

"I own two clothing stores in Brooklyn. All name brands like D&G, Prada, Gucci, etc. I also sell jewelry and own a car dealership. Business is good, I can't complain."

I still wasn't impressed. Everyone I knew had a store, especially t-shirts.

He was brief, never going into detail, making me wish I hadn't asked my next question. Hopefully, he would blame it on the champagne talking, and not me.

"Do you sell drugs?" I blurted out, ready to end everything now if that's what he did. The way he threw that money on the counter at the bookstore reminded me of someone that hustled, and I didn't want to compete with the streets anymore. It was a wild life I didn't want to live.

"No!" he said laughing, "I got a bachelors degree in

Business from NYU."

"That doesn't mean you don't hustle, it just means you're smarter."

"No, Oshyn, I don't sell drugs. I never have and never will," he said, raising his right hand to God. I wasn't convinced.

"And if I did," he continued, "you think I'd be stupid enough to tell you?"

"You'd be surprised," I said, recounting all the niggas that bragged openly about hustling.

"So, what were your thoughts while you were staring me down at church?" he asked, out of nowhere.

*Oh shit, he did see me,* I thought, as I tried to think of a quick come back. It seemed like a cat had my tongue because I couldn't think of anything to say. I was so embarrassed that he brought it up, I wanted to crawl under the table. Besides, the thought of his naked body had me wet.

"It's okay," he said, trying to reassure me. "All the girls from Rochester stare at us Brooklyn boys that way."

I laughed hard at his comment. I was caught red handed and didn't have a defense. I loosened up as we talked a bit more, and laughed at his jokes for the rest of the night. He had a great sense of humor.

"What makes you happy?" he asked.

"What makes me happy?" I repeated to myself out loud. I paused and thought hard about the question. I was trying to remember if anyone had ever asked me about my happiness before. "I love to write, mainly poems though. It's something other than my son that I've fallen in love with. It's a way out of this crazy world, my release. I hope one day I have the courage to make a book out of the poetry I've written."

"I used to go to spoken word events all the time in Brooklyn. Can I hear one of your poems?" he asked, apparently interested in my hobby.

"No, it's too personal. I don't want to be judged because of my past."

"I won't judge you."

"That's what they all say."

We enjoyed each other's conversation a bit more while we ate our food and ordered dessert.

"Can I see you tomorrow?" he asked, wasting no time.

"I don't know, I might be busy," I said, still not wanting to seem too available. "I have a lot of closings to handle. Call me though, I'll see what I can do."

He leaned in my direction and pressed his soft moist lips against my cheek.

"You'll make time," he said, hypnotizing me again with his gray eyes. I smiled again, knowing I would.

# 7

# *CHLOE*

"Chloe, I need to see you," was all he said when I picked up the phone.

"You know that my time is valuable, and calling me at the last minute is unacceptable." My tone with him was harsh and reprimanding. He loved to be talked to like a small child who was in trouble. He was just another man with too much money in his pockets and time on his hands. "Where are you?" I asked him, wondering how far he wanted me to travel for my services this time.

"I'm in Miami. My pilot is waiting to pick you up. Where are you?"

"You know I don't usually tell my location, but if you must know I'm in D.C." *Umh,* I thought, *I'm charging him an extra two g's for that information.*

"What are you doing in D.C.?" he asked.

"Look, you're getting a little too personal. Our

relationship is strictly business, nothing more!"

"Fair enough," he responded like a sucker. "Are you coming?"

"You got my money, right?"

"Of course. I'll see you when you arrive."

I hung up the phone, thinking about the first time I met Deshawn Simmons. It was last year when I was on an all-expense paid trip to Denver, Colorado with another one of my clients. I had been out all day enjoying the unpredictable ski slopes and had decided to go back to my room and warm up when Deshawn caught my eye. Even through the bone chilling cold air, my body had hot flashes as I watched his dark sexy ass talking to a couple of white men. His hooded black mink coat, loosely hugged his six foot seven inch body. He was so tall it looked like he was walking on stilts. The diamond that hung from his ear was so large and bright, that my stare was limited from the light that shined in my eyes. It had to be fifteen carats, easy.

I noticed him drooling over me, so I kept walking. I remembered thinking that whoever he was, he had a lot of money, obviously by the company he kept. I had taken a big chance by just walking away from him, but it was all part of a bigger plan. My stock value had always skyrocketed considerably when I seemed uninterested. I felt his eyes watching me while I headed back into my five-star hotel room. I knew, without a doubt, that we'd meet again and that's when I planned on making my move.

Later on that night, I escorted my client to this huge charity event that he was hosting. There were over five hundred people there, all high-powered CEO's. I hung on his arm for almost the whole night, while he greeted his guest, until I saw Deshawn sitting at a table holding, what looked to be a mini press conference. The cameras surrounded him, flashing their bright lights, while someone gave him an interview. I had to know what the fuck was going on.

I excused myself from my date and walked, like a model, over toward him. I could tell by his reaction that the five-carat diamond necklace stunned him. I slipped him my number and noticed the wedding band that caressed his finger. For not one second did I utter a word, and when my job was done, I walked away, knowing his eyes watched my ass once again.

When the event was over, I went back to the room while my date said the rest of his goodbyes to the generous donators. Just as I was looking up his salary on the internet, my phone rang. The caller ID read unknown caller. I smiled to myself, knowing it was Deshawn, before I even picked up the phone. Curiosity always kills the cat.

We talked for a while, and he explained to me that he played pro ball for Miami Heat, which explained the height. I wasn't much of a sports fan, but he felt the need to tell me that he was a starter. I'm not sure if it was the liquor talking, but he also mentioned renegotiating another endorsement deal for an extra five to ten million a year. I knew at that point he would be on the Chloe long-term list.

I figured that was enough reminiscing, and decided to go to the location where his pilot was waiting on me. When I pulled up, I hopped out of the car like a movie star, and boarded the private jet that was exclusively for me. I made it my business to indulge in the caviar and champagne while we lifted off.

The plane ride gave me a chance to relax and just think about life. I looked out the window at the clear dark night and was relieved that, out of anger, I didn't spend the money I was saving. I hated for Oshyn to feel like she had the upper hand, but I had to. It was all part of a bigger plan. It took all I had inside of me not to just throw the black duffle bag full of money in her face, but I remained calm, agreeing to leave her house without a fight.

I told Oshyn that I was moving into a house that Joy was building in Raleigh when, in fact, it was *my* fifty-five hundred square foot brick domain that was being built. When she asked how Joy came into all that money, I told her that it was an inheritance and she stopped questioning me. I had to stick to my intent to live like a millionaire was supposed to live when the time was right. Even though it didn't seem like it, I had control again. The house was to be finished in seven more months, so I had to figure out what to do until then.

The plane landed safely two hours later, and my client's driver met me.

"Hello, Madame Chloe," he said, as he guided me into the White Phantom. "Lovely seeing you again."

Deshawn always hired the best, and he paid good too, dishing out three thousand dollars a night or more, depending on how rough we got. The driver wasted no time taking me straight to his condo on South Beach, and escorted me straight up to the Presidential Suite, where I had a hot bubble bath waiting for me. Honey suckle, cantaloupe, strawberries and grapes lined the edge of the twenty-carat, gold-rimmed bathtub. I inspected the room and noticed a glass of white wine on the bathroom counter that was stained with red lipstick.

"Deshawn!" I called out, wondering what was going on. Another woman was not part of the plan and didn't fit his regular routine.

I eased up a bit, figuring he ran out for something, which wasn't unusual, and began undressing. The room was steamy and the mirrors were a little foggy, which meant someone had just gotten out the shower. The music system played Luther Vandross' greatest hits very softly in the background.

I slipped into the steamy hot water and closed my eyes for a while, until I heard the sound of heels clicking on the marble floor. I sat up as the sound stopped at the bathroom door. Before me stood a white woman, slightly older, who was maybe in her early forties. She brushed her long strawberry blonde hair out of her face, and stared at me like she was ready for war.

I stood up out the water quickly, leaving my body dripping with suds everywhere. I looked around and didn't see anything close enough to use as a weapon. At first, I thought she was a deranged fan that had somehow snuck in his hotel room, but there was something about her that made me think differently. Whatever the case, she was getting ready to get her ass beat. She didn't strike me as a fighter, but I never underestimated anybody, especially a white woman. Her silence, and the way she stared at me, put me more on defense than anything else. She watched as I found my weapon of choice, the empty wine bottle and picked it up slowly.

"Please, sit back down. I just wanted to know where my husband was going when he said he had to work," she said, sipping the new glass of wine she had in her hand. "Here is fifteen thousand dollars. I want to see what it is that he leaves his family for."

*Wife?* I thought to myself. I knew he was married, but he never told me it was to a white woman. I should have figured though. If she had been a black bitch, blood would've been splattered all over this bathroom by now. There would've been no talking. "Umh…" *The nigga got a little extra cash and switched sides. It was becoming more and more common.*

The woman took off the black teddy she was wearing, and revealed a body that mimicked a twenty year old. She was in perfect shape, built like Tina Turner. As she placed her wine beside the tub, she climbed in the water, surprisingly still wearing her Gucci heals.

With my money on the counter, I didn't ask any questions, and proceeded to make my way toward her. I straddled her roughly, and started kissing on her neck, letting my fingers wander around her small frame. I slipped them under the water and began playing with her pussy until she let out a slight gasp.

"Mmmmm," she moaned. Her size D breasts, that she paid a fortune for, sat up perfectly while I licked them. Her glassy eyes were a sign that she was in ecstasy. I inched her body out of the water, and placed her on her back. "Ahhh, fuck!" she shouted, as I began to lick her clit with soft sensuous strokes. I was just about to turn her out when we heard the door close.

I jumped up and asked, "Who the fuck is that?"

"Probably Deshawn. He doesn't know I'm here right now, but it doesn't matter. Nothing matters anymore." She pulled me back close to her with force, and wrapped her thin lips around my tits.

"What in the hell is going on here?" Deshawn asked, ready to shit on his self in disbelief. He couldn't believe his wife and mistress were fucking each other.

Neither of us said a word as she continued to roam my body with her mouth. When I opened my eyes from the pleasure she was giving me, I noticed Deshawn pouting miserably on the side. He was so confused that he didn't know whether to be angry, or to run from being caught.

I got off of her, and headed his way, still soaking wet from the water I never dried off my body. I left a trail of small soapy puddles behind me. I took baby steps, careful not to slip on the wet marble floor, and walked straight up to him. Within seconds, I had yanked his pants down to the floor. I grabbed his well-endowed dick into my hands and nibbled on his nuts until he couldn't stand straight. I wanted to feel his big dick in my mouth, but had gotten impatient with all the excitement, and decided that I just wanted him inside of me.

I pushed him on the floor, with his pants still wrapped around his ankles and hopped on his dick. I rode it for a while, feeling my pussy getting wetter with every stroke. I slid my finger a little into his ass hole, forgetting that his wife was still here. I smiled. *Looks like I have salvaged a boring marriage, and gained two clients for life.*

# 8

# OSHYN

A few weeks had passed since I saw Brooklyn, and I could barely get him out of my mind. He called a few times, but I purposefully didn't answer. My work kept me swamped, and I really didn't have any time to play. I'm sure I could have made time, but the whole situation of having a man in my life had me feeling a little uneasy. I wasn't supposed to be enjoying his company this much, and found myself stopping in the middle of my day to wonder where he was, and what he was doing. I left myself vulnerable to him, which is not where I wanted to be, and was subconsciously sabotaging whatever could've existed between us.

I'd gotten myself comfortable in my bed, ready to call it a night when my phone rang. "Hello?"

"Hey stranger, it's Brooklyn," he said. "What's up? Is everything okay with you? I haven't heard from you in a while. I was starting to get a little worried."

"Nah...everything has been straight. I've been real busy, that's all."

"Oh...okay, Ma. I'd really like to see you tonight, if that's cool with you."

"I don't know," I said, looking at the clock. It was already ten and I had to be up by six-thirty. "It's a little too late. Maybe tomorrow."

"Nooooooo!" Brooklyn moaned. "I got something special planned. I won't keep you up too late, I promise."

I debated briefly on his offer. I desperately needed some excitement in my life and could use a good surprise. Part of me wanted to know what he had in store on a Wednesday night, and plus I kind of missed talking to him since our first date. I finally agreed to see him, and he told me where to meet him.

I hopped out of bed, threw on some black jeans and a white shirt, and headed into the living room.

"Hey, Chloe," I said, interrupting her TV program. "Can you watch Micah for me while I step out for a minute?"

"Where you going?" she asked with an attitude, as she looked me up and down.

I was amazed at her nerve. "Do I ask you where you're going when you float in and out of town?" I stood with my hands on my hips, waiting for her anticipated stupid response. She looked at me like she hated me for some reason. I ignored her nastiness, reminding myself it was probably because of the tragic loss of her mother. I eased up a bit. "I'm going out with the dude I met at the bookstore. I'm not staying out for a long time, so can you watch Micah for me? Pleaseeeeee," I begged. "He's already asleep."

"That nigga really got your nose wide open if you're leaving the crib on a work day." Chloe rolled her eyes.

"I didn't ask you for all of that," I said, aggravated that our conversation had carried on for this long. "Yes or no?"

"Yeah, I'll watch him," she said, as I walked out the door. "Make sure your square ass puts on a condom," she added, with a loud laugh.

*Does she call that advice,* I thought to myself. I drove to a parking lot in Mini City, where Brooklyn wanted us to meet. On the way, I wondered would I ever get married, and what it would be like to share my life with someone who wasn't into playing games. All of the men I'd ever dated amounted to nothing. I guess that's why with Brooklyn, my guards were up.

As I pulled into the lot, I mumbled to myself, "He better not be late this…"

Before I could complete my sentence, I saw Brooklyn pull up in his sparkling black 2007 Range Rover. I couldn't help but feel sixteen again. It felt as though I was going out on my first date. When I climbed into the truck, the smell of his Black Ice car freshener pierced my nose.

"I missed you," he said, rubbing his hand on mine.

I pulled it away quickly, not interested in his display of affection. "Whatever, where are we going?"

"Just sit back and relax. We'll be there in a second."

Ten minutes later, we finally pulled up at a small club downtown. The spot appeared to be well kept and a slightly older crowd.

"I don't like clubs," I whined, while he opened my door.

"Chill," he said. "Just chill." We walked in, and I examined the place as we took our seats. I turned my attention to the stage as a heavyset woman read a poem about the trials of being a single parent. The crowd roared with laughter as she made light of her difficult situation. I looked at Brooklyn and smiled. "So you like?" he asked, already knowing the answer.

"I love, thank you! How did you know about this place?" I wondered, looking at what seemed to be at least two hundred people in the cramped space. On a Wednesday night in Raleigh, I thought that was pretty odd.

"Believe it or not, I enjoy poetry too. I've never performed though. I just like to write and listen to other people flow. It's so crazy because I never met a woman who shares my same interests."

His comment sent a message to my heart, because the feelings were mutual. We sat back for a while, drinking white wine and getting lost again in each other's company. I felt like I had known Brooklyn for an eternity as we shared an intimate and stimulating conversation. My heartbeat got faster as I hung on to every word he said. His conversation was so versatile that I was surprised as to how much we had in common. We went from politics to sports to Wall Street, all in the same sentence.

He kept his promise by returning me to my car within a couple of hours. Not really wanting to end the night, we ended up sitting in the car and admiring the stars and full moon that sat over us.

"Are you married?" I asked Brooklyn, catching him off guard.

I was beginning to feel like everything was too good to be true and that there had to be a catch. He took my breath away with his looks, made me blush with his stare, and dampened my panties with one glance of his smile. To me, there was no way that he was still available. Something had to be up.

"Married?" he repeated offensively. "No, I'm not married. What are you talking about?"

"Then what's the problem? Why aren't you involved with someone...or are you?" I asked, trying to get him to confess.

"No, I'm not involved with anyone, I'm just like you...I *choose* to be single. I was dating a woman for a minute, but I found that she just sucked all my energy from me." I listened closely as he continued. "I carry a lot of obligations on my shoulders as far as my businesses are concerned, so I finally realized that I need a woman in my life who is trying to help me, not hinder me."

"Why do you feel she was holding you back?" I asked, genuinely wanting to know.

"She wanted too much of my time and I didn't have it to give. Well, maybe I didn't want to give it. All she wanted to do was spend my money, which don't get me wrong, it's no big deal. I believe that a man is responsible for making his woman happy. If money does that, then it's fine, but there has to be a balance. She was emptying my account *and* complaining about me never being around. I gave her the option to never lift a finger, which left her most of the time with nothing to do. She didn't understand that if both of us sat around the house all day and chilled, no one was going to have any money to spend."

"So, what you're saying is, you created a monster?"

"Basically, but I've learned from my mistakes, which answers your question," he said, in a sarcastic tone.

I wondered if he was serious about everything he said, or if he was just talking out of his ass. "Money seems to always be a problem in all relationships. Maybe if she had her own money, the two of you would've made it."

"I've learned that money isn't everything. At the time, I was young and getting money. That basically took precedence over my life. I'm pretty sure I could've made it work between us, but in my heart I knew she wasn't the one for me. Now since I've matured, I want a woman in my life who has her own goals and dreams for the future. And not only that, I want her to be taking steps toward making that happen. I want my wife by my side helping me to build our empire, not tearing it down. She needs to be an asset, not a liability. Oshyn, I think that woman is you."

Whoa, was all I could think. I sat in awe at Brooklyn's take on relationships. Most of the niggas I knew didn't care if the bitch graduated high school, much less if she had a goal or two. And if she did, it was to get the nigga with the deepest pockets. And all that talk about me being the one...well, too much for one night.

We talked a little more and decided to end the night. He insisted that I not step out the car until he opened the door for me. *I could get used to being treated like a queen*, I thought, as he walked me back to my car.

"I had a really nice time," I said to him, as he stepped closer to me, invading my breathing zone.

"I did too. Thank you," Brooklyn said, as he reached over and kissed me on my forehead. I was surprised and flattered that he hadn't gone for the lips. He was proving himself to be a real gentleman. He opened my car door and patiently waited while I got in. "Please don't wait that long again until you answer my calls. I won't take up too much of your time, I just want to know if you're okay."

"Okay," I said, blushing. It was nice to know that he

wondered about me as much as I did about him.

We both drove away, going our separate ways once again. Although I had a great time, I was tired and had a long day ahead of me.

When I returned home, to my surprise I opened the door, only to see Chloe's naked ass holding her cell phone in one hand and playing with my dildo in the other. At first glance, I thought I was crazy. Chloe had apparently created an outline of a whip cream bra that was creamy and stood up off her chest.

"What are you doing? And where is Micah?" I screamed.

"Can you lower your voice, I'm on an important phone call with one of my clients?" Chloe's tone was calmer than usual.

"Bitch, what do you mean lower my voice! You're supposed to be watching my son, but instead you're having phone sex!" My eyes darted over to the can of whip cream on the counter, and then back to the dildo. "And who told you to go in my room?"

"Oshyn, are you mad that I found your little friend? Just be glad it's not your real man."

"Chloe, just know the only reason why I put up with your shit is because of a promise I made to my mother." I turned around, not allowing her to respond, realizing I hadn't checked on Micah.

Within seconds, I opened the door to peek in on my little angel. Luckily he was fast asleep, not even able to comprehend how crazy his cousin really was. After all the drama, I jumped in my bed, hoping to have sweet dreams. *I knew I should have asked Apples to watch Micah,* I chanted, before pulling the covers over my head.

The morning had come faster than expected. It was seven-fifteen, and getting out of bed felt like a task, in and of itself.

*Too much to drink last night,* I thought, as my head spun around the room. I drug myself out the bed to get Micah, and we both got dressed. As we walked downstairs, Chloe was in the kitchen flipping pancakes.

"Hey, little man. You want something to eat?" she said.

"Ooooh, pancakes. Yes, I want some," Micah answered.

"Good morning, Sunshine," Chloe said to me, with a devilish grin.

I shot her a dirty look, letting her know that I wasn't going to entertain her childish games, especially in front of my son. I was really starting to think the bitch was skitzo.

"Micah, we're running late, baby. Mommy will take you to McDonalds on the way to Grandma's," I said.

"Yeah," Micah said, running towards the door.

"Chloe, we're gone," I said.

"Hey, if you stop by the mall on the way from work, can you buy me those new Dolce and Gabbana shades and Guiseppe Zanotti sandals? I think there only like sixteen hundred." Chloe said, nonchalantly. "I've got somewhere to go tonight."

*I can't believe she just asked me that,* I thought. "No, I'll buy you a newspaper so you can get your lazy ass a job. You are twenty-five, don't you want more out of life than what you are already doing? You got five hundred thousand dollars when you were twenty-one. Not twenty thousand dollars, but half a million, and you blew it."

I was frustrated at her lack of ambition and recent mooching off of me. I had agreed to let her stay with me for a couple of months until Joy's house was finished, but now it was time for her to go.

"These niggas is my job, and as long as they tricking they paper, I'll never work. Fuck you!"

"Well, your pussy ain't charging enough because apparently you're fucking for pennies. You don't even have enough money to buy your own crib, so you have to stay with your homegirl."

"You don't know what I got, so keep my business out of your mouth."

"You're a stupid bitch, and as long as you're in my house, everything you do is my business! Matter of fact, get the FUCK out!" I said, slamming the door.

I was sick of Chloe's ass. She inherited all of that money from her mother's life insurance policy, and had absolutely nothing to show for it. She even told me that the three hundred thousand dollar house she once owned was foreclosed on because she had run out of money to pay the mortgage, so that's why she came to town. We never got along and I guess never will. *What a waste of a person*, I thought, while I buckled Micah in his seatbelt, wishing that I could transform her into someone else. I wished I could offer her a job with me, but family and business didn't mix.

When I reached my grandmother's house, Apples had already dropped Bella off. As my administrative assistant, her responsibility was to open the office, and she was always prompt. I was so glad to have Apples as my best friend. She proved to be so responsible.

"Hola, Mama," I said, kissing my grandmother's aging cheek as I walked in the house. It was Spanish custom.

"Hola, baby," she said, in her thick Spanish accent. The aroma of rice -arroz y pollo saturated the house. She was always cooking.

I looked around at the many photographs that lined the shelves. The majority of them were of my mother. I walked over and picked up the gold 8x10 frame.

"Mama, how old was Mommy in this picture?" I asked.

She stopped stirring her industrial sized pot of rice and came over to observe.

"Oh, she was ju age in dis picture. Beautiful, beautiful girl she was, ju look just like her." I smiled at the thought of our resemblance. My childhood with her was slim, so I was happy to look at a picture of her every chance I got. The smile on her face was so innocent in the picture, never expecting her life to turn out how it did. I missed her dearly, we both did.

I put the picture back, noticing there weren't any of Aunt Mahogany on the shelves. I decided not to ask why. If she was anything like her daughter, Chloe, I understood.

My grandmother was a devout Christian. The virtuous woman the bible speaks about in Proverbs thirty-one. She was my hero.

"How ju doing?" she asked, always knowing the answer.

"I'm good, Mama. Business is good, I'm happy again."

"Who is he?"

"Who is who?"

"The man?" she asked, with a serious look.

"What man?"

She always knew. "Don't get stupid with me."

"How do you know these things?" I laughed.

"A gift from God."

*That's some gift*, I thought. But she was right. I remember telling her when I lost my virginity to Trent at sixteen. That day when I came home and greeted her with a kiss like I always did, she immediately grabbed my hand, looked me in the eyes and said, "Ju had sex today, didn't ju? I see it in jur eyes." To this day, I don't know how she knew.

"That's some gift." I shook my head. "His name is Brooklyn. I saw him at church two Sundays ago, but we actually met at the mall. We've dated a couple of times, and he seems nice. Men are always nice on the first date, right."

"Baby, be careful," she warned. "Watch jur associations. People aren't always how they seem, and distance jurself from Chloe. I know she's mi granddaughter too, but she means ju no good. She just popped up out of nowhere, which makes me wonder."

"She spent all her money, that's all," I told Grandma, trying to ease her mind. She didn't need to get all worked up and have her blood pressure rise over Chloe.

Grandma was so wise and had so much information to share. She always made me feel like she knew something about Chloe that I didn't. Their relationship changed ever since Grandma had suffered the mild heart attack when I was in the hospital. She never told me what happened, just always warned me to stay away. I knew what she was saying about Chloe was true, but she was still family, my blood. I felt like I could change her, and that maybe some of my motivation would rub off on her. So far it hasn't.

"When are you coming to church with me again?" That was a question she asked everyday.

"Soon Grandma, I promise." I hated lying to her.

"Soon may never come, baby, soon may never come," she said, as she walked away humming an old gospel hymn.

Sometimes I thought that my grandma was senile, but she was wise beyond words. She was an incredible woman. Meeting Joe Turner, my grandfather, as a teenager gave her more than she could handle. They say opposites attract, and she and my granddad were very different.

Grandma had just moved to the States from Rio Piedra, Puerto Rico, and spoke very little English. My granddad, a big time gangsta, saw something special in her, and took time from the streets to teach her his language. Obviously he taught her a little too much, because a few months later, she became pregnant with my Aunt Mahogany. My great grandparents were outraged. Not only did she get pregnant at a young age, but that she had gotten pregnant by a black man. She was kicked out of her parent's house and moved into an apartment with Joe.

One year later, she got pregnant with my mom, but unfortunately when she was eight months pregnant, Joe was kidnapped and found dead in front of my grandma's doorstep. To this day no one knows what happened. They never got a chance to marry.

After his death, grandma was no longer naïve, and had learned a few things from Joe about 'the game.' She did what it took to feed her family, and sacrificed a lot...even her body.

Maybe we understood each other so well because of our spirit. I wasn't quite grown and she was old enough to know that nothing really mattered. There was a fifty-year age difference between us, yet she was my closest friend. She was someone that I knew wouldn't judge me. She may not have agreed with my choices, but she never judged.

"Oh well, I'm off to work. Thanks for the advice," I said, kissing her on the cheek once again.

"Anytime, baby," she said. Just as I walked out the door, Micah and Bella ran pass me at top speed. "Micah, stop running in this house!" I shouted. "Don't worry, Grandma, he only has a few weeks left before school starts."

"Leave my baby alone. He's not bothering me," she said.

I walked out the house shaking my head because she spoiled him rotten, but that's another reason why I loved her so much.

❀　❀　❀

I arrived at the office at eight-thirty, and was greeted by an overload of phone calls in my inbox to return. I had just negotiated a deal with a developer who was building one hundred three-story town homes and agreed to let my company, *Oshyn Realty*, sell them. They had just started breaking ground, and the prices were extremely low in a rapidly growing area of Raleigh. The town homes were sure to make my company a twenty thousand dollar profit, so I was very excited.

All the calls were from customers wanting to make offers on the properties. I had a lot of work to do, so I walked down the hall into my office, and saw five huge boxes stacked high. I hated clutter.

"Brian," I called out to my agent. "What's this?"

"I don't know. They were delivered this morning. I was wondering the same thing," he said smiling.

Brian was tall, white and handsome. He looked like someone straight out of a Calvin Klein ad, and was a selling guru.

"Hand me a box cutter," I said, to anyone who was listening.

Apples came from nowhere with the tool. *I had some nosey workers*, I thought, as I opened one of the boxes. Tears instantly welled up in my eyes when I saw what sat inside. There were nearly fifty books in this one box. Urban fiction, romance, poetry, real estate, you name it, and it was there. I opened the card that was taped to the top book, which read:

> *Brooklyn's Oshyn,*
> *I hope this has made you as happy as you've made me the moment I met you.*
> > *Love,*
> > *Your Future*

I sat back and smiled. I had given up on love and didn't think a man could be so sweet. This was the best gift in the world, and something that touched my heart so deeply. It was still only the beginning, and I was doing something I swore I would never do again. I was falling in love.

# 9

# OSHYN

"Do you believe in love at first sight?" I asked my grandma, as she swept the dust from the sidewalk. I sat on the porch, picking the peddles off the flowers in her garden.

"Why? Ju think ju in love?" she asked, slapping the flower out my hand.

"I don't know. I'm not even sure if I know what love is anymore." I lowered my head, trying my best to hide the tears that welled up in my eyes.

No matter how tough I portrayed myself to be, deep down inside I just wanted to be loved. I never gave anyone the chance though. The wall I built left no room for trust, only bitterness. Over the years, it had grown so high that even I couldn't see over it.

"No, No, No!" she said, putting her broom down and taking a seat next to me. "Ju do know what love is? It's patient, it's kind, it keeps no records of wrongs, it..."

"That's just not realistic," I interrupted. "Love hurts…"

"No, get that out of jur mind. Jur mind is a powerful tool, and that thought is deteriorating jur body. Love is all the things the Bible seys it is, and ju deserve to be loved that way and no other. Love doesn't hurt. It was never meant to. People hurt people but love, true love NEVER hurts."

I sighed, putting my head on her frail shoulder. She rubbed my hair, soothing my broken heart and asked, "Who? Who ju think ju in love with…this Brooklyn boy?"

"Yeah, it's the same guy that I've been telling you about. We've been going out for a couple of weeks now, and I still don't know him well, but I think he's the one. I just feel it." I looked into her mysterious eyes and hoped she had an answer to my unknown question.

"Baby, not everything we desire is good for us, neither all that we cherish is pleasing to God. Seek God's grace first. Ask for His guidance and He will reveal it to ju."

I gave her a hug, not quite understanding what she meant, but took the advice to heart anyway. She was a very spiritual woman, and although she didn't want us to make bad decisions, she stood to the side while we made our own choice.

My attention turned to the loud music coming down the street. The beats of Yung Joc echoed like steel drums, which sent Micah and Bella running to do the infamous motorcycle dance. I smiled at first, until I realized it was Chloe with the loud music.

She pulled up in front of the house sporting her brand new 2007 Infiniti truck that one of her boyfriends must have bought her. 'The Power of Pussy' she would say, 'The Risk of AIDS' I would say.

I was never one to judge, or at least tried real hard not too, but Chloe fucked anyone with money, and her method of protection was abortion. I'm not sure if she knew how many she had or if she even really cared. I once told her that she needed a lifetime membership to Planned Parenthood. She laughed, but I didn't mean it to be funny.

She hopped out of the car, looking like she was headed to the club in a short dress that fell just below her butt cheeks. She greeted Grandma with a kiss like life was swell. Chloe picked up Micah and smothered him with hugs and kisses. It bothered me the way he hugged her back, he obviously loved her.

"Hey," she finally said to me, with Micah still in her arms. "I got all my stuff out the house."

"Where did you go?" I asked, acting concerned. I was still mad at her for the stunt she pulled at my house.

"I moved in with this dude named Beef."

"Didn't you just meet him?" I questioned.

"Yeah, but it doesn't matter because I have no other place to go." She shot me a guilty look and added, "Plus, he just bought me this car," she said, imitating Vanna White.

"That sounds wonderful," I said, trying to appear happy for her.

"Look, I'm sorry for what happened between us. That's your crib and you let me stay there. I didn't respect that. We've been through a lot together, and I don't want to beef with you. We grew up like sisters, so I want to apologize."

I looked into her eyes as she hugged me tightly, trying to piece together her motive. It had been three weeks since I put her out, and this was our first encounter. Either she was sincere, which I doubted, or she needed something soon, which was the case most of the time.

"It's okay," I said, accepting her apology.

"You want to go out later tonight, maybe barhop…talk? Just you and me," she asked.

That was code for me to leave Apples at home. Chloe never said it, but she hated Apples. Even though Chloe and I were raised together at a young age, Apples and I were more like sisters than best friends.

When I moved Apples here, I started spending most of my time with her, and began distancing myself away from Chloe when she came around. Her character wasn't good, her motives were wrong, and her judgments were bad. She was a gold digging whore, and a weight in my road to success. I allowed her to come back because she was my flesh and blood, nothing else.

"Sure," I said, looking at my watch. "Look, I've got to get back to the office and finish up some paperwork. I probably will not be done until late, but call me."

"Okay," she said, hugging me one more time. "No matter what, you know you're my cousin for life."

"Yeah, I know. I feel the same way."

❀   ❀   ❀

I put my head down on my desk in disbelief that I had so much work to do. The papers piled on my glass desk gave me an instant headache just from looking at them.

"Oshyn," Brain said, handing me a Starbucks Double Espresso. "We have so many people signing contracts on new homes. Seventeen more for the week and we're finished! I still can't believe that we're the only two people making commission on all of that money!" he said, a little too excited.

It was a big deal though. At three percent commission, we both grossed in a little over one hundred and fifty thousand dollars in seven months.

"Didn't you buy a couple of properties?" he asked, wondering how much money I had invested in the project.

"Yeah. I bought three town homes, and I just finished a credit check for the renters. They came up squeaky-clean and my tenants will be moving in soon."

Brian and I were the same age, but he was financially illiterate. Although he made a lot of money, he spent most of it on chicken heads and fancy cars, leaving him high and dry until he sold more houses. I, on the other hand, taught myself the proper way to handle my money. I wanted to be rich, and I wasn't getting there by spending it all.

We worked nonstop and were down to the last few contracts when Brian said, "Oshyn, the phone is for you."

"It rang?" I asked.

"Yup, loud and clear," he said, handing me the receiver.

"Good evening, this is Oshyn speaking," I said, wondering who was calling me after working hours.

"Hey, Oshyn, it's Brooklyn."

"How did you get this number?" I asked, knowing I didn't give it to him.

"Well, hello to you too! I tried calling your cell, but it kept going to voicemail, so I called 411 and got the number to Oshyn's Realty. Hope you don't mind, but I just wanted to see you again." He sounded so innocent, like he really meant what he said.

"You're sort of like a stalker," I said half joking.

"I sort of feel like one. Can I see you tonight?"

"Um…yeah, sure. Where?"

"I'm cooking at my crib."

"You cook?" I asked surprised.

"When I'm in the mood, but I'll cook for you anytime."

"Alright. I'll call you when I'm on the way for directions," I said.

He stopped me one last time to play lover boy a few more minutes. We hung up the phone after discussing the specifics about the evening. I tried my best to get back to work, but after three minutes of aimlessly shuffling papers around, I finally stopped. It seemed that since our conversation had ended, my concentration just dwindled away. I put my head down on my over occupied desk and wondered when I had gotten so open.

Usually I wouldn't have even let the thought slither into my mind of play before work, but today I was making an exception. I had hours of intense paperwork to do, but I choose to break one of my most important rules: Money over niggas. Instead of keeping my mind focused on running my business, I was trying to figure out what outfit I was going to wear over Brooklyn's house. I wondered what would keep his eyes glued to me all night. For the first time in a long time, I wanted to make a man happy.

*This might be the night that I wouldn't be home to tuck in Micah.* I felt a little guilty because of my recent absence from my son, but quickly pacified myself with the thought of a romantic night with Brooklyn. *He'll be asleep anyway*, I said to myself, trying to make what I was doing all right. I was so use to dedicating my life to him that I forgot about making me happy.

❋  ❋  ❋

I got to his house around ten, surprisingly impressed by his brick domain that was literally fit for a king. The dimly lit marble walkway led you to his humongous French doors. The moment I approached, he opened the door and greeted me with a warm smile.

"Welcome to mi casa," he said grinning. "You like?"

"I love," I said, admiring his expensive art collection. "This is beautiful." I walked away and helped myself to a tour. "You live alone?" I asked, impressed with the size of the house.

"Yep. For now."

"The store business is better than I thought," I said, surprised that he had acquired all of this. *This house has to be worth half a million easy*, I thought, doing a quick bootleg appraisal.

"Yeah, like I said before, I can't complain."

My phone rang, startling me. I fumbled around for it, realizing that I had forgotten to turn the ringer down. It was Chloe.

"What's up?" I asked her.

"I'm ready to head out. What spot you want to go to?"

"Damn, I forgot all about that. I made plans with Brooklyn, the dude from the bookstore and I'm already at his crib. My bad."

"Oh," she said pissed. "A'ight."

CLICK!

Our brief conversation was over.

"Overbooking dates?" he asked sarcastically.

"That was my cousin and she doesn't count."

"Oh, the girl I saw you with."

"Yeah, her."

He led me to his modern country designed kitchen, where he'd been preparing his feast. It was surrounded by rich cherry wood cabinetry and a four-sided island in the center, which was placed on steel pipe columns. The counter tops were distinctive black and white granite with flecks of red that shot through.

"What are we eating?" I asked, rubbing my hands together ready to dig in.

"Wild salmon, brushed with a honey butter glaze, and white rice mixed with zucchini and squash." He opened the oven to let me peek at his masterpiece.

"You didn't make this," I said, in disbelief. The sweet aroma paralyzed my nose.

"Yes, I did," he said, sensing I wouldn't believe him. "I promise."

We sat down at the dining room table and enjoyed a romantic candle lit dinner with a bottle of vintage white wine. He really did know how to treat a lady. The tunes of Sade that played through the house system, echoed in my ear. I felt like I was the star in a movie.

After dinner, we made ourselves comfortable in the living room. The lighting was brilliant, the mood poetic. The cold leather from the couch, mixed with my drink, made my goose bumps rise again. This was becoming a regular.

"You go to church often?" I asked, reminded by the chandelier hanging at his front door. It was very similar to the one that I had seen there.

"Yeah, I'm trying to get my life right. I just started going to church when I moved here, and I've been going regularly since. I never thought I'd enjoy being taught the word so much."

"Wow!" I said, somewhat speechless. I was a little surprised that my pussy was throbbing for a God fearing man. "So are you saved?"

"Yes," he said confidently. "I'm saved, but it's hard being that way everyday…flesh is weak. I win some days, lose most, but I'm still fighting. How about you? Are you saved?"

"I think so."

"You think so? What does that mean?"

"It means…what does saved mean anyway?" I asked, getting defensive. "No one is perfect, everyone is tempted, and most succumb, so tell me, who is *really* saved? I believe in God, and he knows my heart. I pray with have good intentions, and I think that's enough."

I took another sip of wine and shifted my position on the couch.

"What do you think about sex?" Brooklyn asked.

"Nothing really. The Bible says that you can't have sex until your married. I've been celibate, but it hasn't been for God. It's been because I haven't had anyone to have sex with."

"Hey, at least you're honest," he said, admiring my bluntness. "How is your son doing?"

The question surprised me, not because he asked, but because he thought about him.

"He's doing fine." I smiled to myself.

"Your dimples are so pretty," he said, hypnotized by the deep dents in my cheeks.

"Thank you."

"What's your idea of fun?" I asked, anxious to learn more about him.

"I love to travel. I've been to Milan, Paris, Africa…all over."

"That's impressive," I said, daydreaming of all the places I wanted to go. "I love the *thought* of traveling, but my business has been so busy that I don't have time to even sleep."

"Looks like I'll have to rescue you." He leaned in a little closer, so close I could feel his breath on my face. "So, Oshyn tell me, where can I take you?"

I paused and thought hard about the question he had just asked me. I couldn't remember anyone asking to take me on a trip before. "I would love to go to Miami. It's something about the beach that turns me on. I love watching the waves, it relaxes me."

"Can I take you there one day?" he asked, interested in my happiness.

"No. Not now. I'm too busy and don't want to be distracted from my business."

"I won't distract you."

"That's what they all say."

"I promise. I'm Brooklyn Jones and my word is my bond. Don't judge me for what those other niggas did to you. Look, I'm going to keep it real with you, I want you, Oshyn. I don't know what it is, and I know we just met but...I want you in my life. It's just...it's just something about you I want to protect."

"Whoa," I said, choking on my drink. "We just met. We've only gone out a few times. Pump your brakes."

"For what? When I see something I want, I go after it."

His loud cell phone interrupted us, vibrating on the glass table. I was glad it interrupted us, because I sort of wanted to lay off the relationship subject. I was feeling him, but didn't want to get too close. I was still afraid.

I excused myself to the bathroom. All those glasses of wine were beginning to run its course through my body, and it had to be released. Before I left the bathroom, I applied my lips with my MAC lip gloss. I walked back into the living room, obviously startling him because the phone had fallen to the floor.

"Hello?" I heard a female voice say from a distance.

"Brooklyn...hello?"

He quickly picked up the phone and disconnected the call.

"It's not nice to keep secrets," I said, sitting back down in my seat.

"I have no secrets."

"Everyone has them," I snapped. "And by the way you hung up on her, she's apparently one of them."

"Ma, she's nothing really. Just the past, and mad that she's not the future."

"Whatever, just know this, you have no reason to lie to me. Please don't ever lie to me."

"I won't."

We talked for so long, we didn't notice how late it had gotten. We shared laughs and discreet touches. His phone danced around on the table a few more times since the hang up, and he finally decided to turn it off completely.

He leaned in and kissed me, letting his moist soft lips rest on mine. My heart started to beat faster. I parted my lips, tempting his tongue to meet mine, and he accepted the invitation. He was a great kisser, very sensual. My pussy was soaked. It had been so long since a man was inside my world. I wasn't sure if I was ready to handle all of this.

BANG! BANG! BANG! BANG! BANG! BANG!

"What the fuck?" Brooklyn said, as he jumped up off the couch. "Who in the hell is banging on my door like that? Who is it?" he screamed.

"It's me, nigga, open the door!" the woman shouted.

"Why in the fuck are you popping up over here?"

"Because I know you got that bitch in there. Why are you doing this to me?" she asked sobbing. "Open up the door before I set her car on fire."

He didn't hesitate to open the door at that point. I guess she was known for sticking to her word. I stood up, preparing myself for what came next. A scorned woman was liable to do anything. My past taught me that. She rocked him in the head as soon as she saw him.

"Shante, calm down," he said, putting her in a headlock. I laughed out loud. Thought it was funny.

"You leave me for that?" she said, referring to me. I didn't say a thing because this wasn't my beef.

"Shante, get the fuck out of here," he said, letting her go. He was mad, maybe more like furious.

She stepped in the house a bit more, allowing the light to reveal her identity. I stood in shock, realizing she was the girl that bumped into me at the mall.

She looked up at me, like Shug looked at Celie in *The Color Purple*, struggling to get her micro-braids out her face. She resembled a crackhead more than the young lady she was supposed to be.

"I'ma fuck you up, bitch!" the girl shouted, as she tried to escape from Brooklyn's grip.

I picked up the empty bottle of wine that was still sitting on the hardwood floor, and threw it as hard as I could at her head.

Brooklyn ducked and released her from his grasp. Instantly the girl slipped and fell to the floor. Just as the shattered glass flew everywhere, I ran over to her, while she was still on the floor. I stomped my foot into her side a couple of times until Brooklyn stopped me.

"I'm not the one for this shit. Don't fuck with me, bitch," I said, never raising my voice. I was still in control, and I wanted both of them to know that.

I crossed my arms and sat on the edge of the couch like nothing ever happened. I was claiming my territory. Shante held her bruised side as she struggled to get up. She had lost the battle and eventually decided to give up.

"This ain't the end," she said, as Brooklyn shoved her out the door, slamming it behind him.

"No secrets, huh?" I said, with a smirk. I wanted to tell him about the prior situation between the girl, now known as Shante, but I chose not to. Our night was going too well and I didn't want to add more drama to the mix.

"No, she's not a secret. Look, Oshyn, I'm sorry about that. I'm not trying to bring no drama in your life. She's nothing, believe that."

"Sure," I said, not caring too much about his plea for forgiveness. "Don't fuck with me, Brooklyn," I warned again, hoping I had showed him that I meant business.

He grabbed me again, sticking his thick tongue in my mouth. This time I didn't fight it. I let my guard down.

It was time.

"Wait!" he said, stopping abruptly. "We can't do this." I just stood there, not really knowing what else to say. "I know it sounds crazy, but I'm falling in love with you. Every girl I've ever been with, I've just fucked. I've never been in love before, but you, you're different. I can't really explain it. The times that we've shared together hold a special place in my heart. So, I want our first time to be special too."

I wanted that day to be today, but I was happy to know that a man actually cared about me and not just my body. It seemed too good to be true, but if my heart was right, he was definitely the one.

# 10

# CHLOE

Brooklyn's taste in women was unusual. I stared him down, clocking the way he greeted the women passing by. Word on the street was that he liked women who went both ways, and it wasn't just a fantasy of his. From what I heard, he only fucked with women into ménage a trios. That's why I was so surprised that he hooked up with Oshyn. *She always gets the good ones,* I thought, as I watched him like a hawk through the thick fog that suffocated the air in the club. He never saw me, but my eyes were locked on him.

We were at The Supper Clubb, the hottest nightclub around. Joy's flight had come in a couple of hours earlier, so she was ready to party hard. I had become a regular at this spot and everybody knew my name. The moment I walked through the door, VIP treatment is what I got. They weren't used to city bitches, so all eyes were on me.

Whoever said that niggas in the south were slow, had

never been to North Carolina. I always assumed they couldn't keep up, but I'd met a few with long money. My ultimate goal was to make my way to Charlotte. I'd heard about their new basketball team, and the players with deep pockets.

The club was jammed packed and bottles were popping everywhere. While the familiar smell of weed filled the air, me and Joy posted up at the VIP bar, ready to roll up a blunt.

"Put that shit up! You know you can't smoke that shit in here," I heard a loud voice say from behind me.

I turned around and saw Eric, the manager of the club, posted up against the wall with some young busted bitch.

"Shut the fuck up," I said to E. "You're gonna go to jail fucking with them little ass girls. Go get me and my bitch something to drink," I ordered. He left and came back with two bottles of Don P. We laughed for a minute and he excused himself back to work.

Brooklyn was talking to an average bitch when I spotted him again. She was giving him hell, with her mouth going a mile a minute. Even though I couldn't hear what was going on, the body language read animosity. With her hands on her hips and her fingers in his face, I could tell that she definitely had a problem. There was nothing special about her either. She wasn't too skinny and not real cute. *She must have given him some amazing head*, I thought, wondering why he was allowing her to make such a scene.

I had been inquiring about Brooklyn on the streets. If Oshyn was falling for him, he needed to be investigated. It was apparent that he lived a flamboyant lifestyle, a lifestyle my cousin knew nothing about. Nights when he wasn't on the phone with her, he was out spending big money on women at the club, and I was getting the full report.

"Here," Joy said, handing me some ecstasy pills and rubbing her hand against my ass. "Take that."

I swallowed the small pill, never taking my eyes off Brooklyn, and waited for it to take effect. She moved her fingers seductively across my bare nipples. They were hard as a rock and my pussy was wet too. No one noticed her fondling me because the smoke machine was on full blast.

Joy was originally from Atlanta. I met her there a year ago doing what I did best. My client was closing a major deal with some businessmen from Tokyo, and he wanted to impress them so he hired two dancers. One of them was Joy. She had one of the sexiest bodies that I'd ever seen; built like a track star. I remember her licking her full lips, never taking her eyes off me. I watched her move seductively through the crowd, stealing everyone's breath away. She accepted no less than one hundred dollar bills from anyone, and made sure her guest left the gathering satisfied.

We exchanged numbers, hoping to get together at a later date. But surprisingly, she called me later on that night and I ended up at her house. She greeted me at the door wearing a red satin robe with nothing underneath. She was one hundred percent feminine, the way I like them. I couldn't stand a butch bitch. What was the point? We didn't talk much on our first encounter, which wasn't necessary anyway. We were there to handle business.

Grabbing me by the hand, she led me into the bedroom, laying me down on her waterbed. I relaxed as I heard the smooth sounds of R. Kelly in the background. She began to undress me and kiss my navel. My body shivered, as I realized she was a master with her tongue. She moved up to my breasts, sucking them until they were swollen. It felt so good. She took off my panties and started licking my shaved pussy.

"Oh, my God!" I screamed, with my eyes rolling in back of my head.

She took long soft strokes between my pussy and clit, making it almost impossible for me to breath. She was definitely a pro, and was moved to the top of my *best fuck* list.

"Open your mouth and suck my cock!" I remembered her demanding with her rubber strap on. She climbed over the top of my face, getting into the perfect position. "Stick your tongue in my pussy," she said, as she rotated her hips against my mouth.

My tongue examined her thick, bald pussy, almost drowning in her wetness. We enjoyed this for hours. Cumming, bathing, cumming, talking, cumming, sleeping...

She wasn't my first and wouldn't be my last. I liked dick and pussy...call it the best of both worlds. Joy was prime meat and I knew it.

When I snapped back from my daydreaming, Brooklyn was still arguing with the bitch in the corner and I was sick of waiting.

"Brooklyn," I said, interrupting their conversation.

"Hey," he said, half-smiling. "Oshyn's cousin, right?"

"Yeah, and I don't think she'd be too happy to see this bitch in your face," I said, daring the broad to say something.

"What?" the bitch said, looking like she was ready to jump. I noticed that she was the bitch from the mall, which really made me ready to beat her ass.

"Shante, get your crazy ass from around me... damn...I'm not fucking with you no more," he said, grabbing her arm and shoving her away like a little girl. She aggravated him and it showed in his tense face. Whoever Shante was, knew how to push his buttons and he allowed it.

Brooklyn excused himself and gave me his undivided attention. "What's up, Ma?"

"Look. I see you out here getting it and I want a piece."

"What...?"

"Seeing as though one of your new girlfriends is my cousin, I figured that you'd look out for *family* and put me on. But don't worry, it'll be between you and me. Strictly business."

I was referring to the big time hustler I found out he was, who moved to Raleigh from an unknown place. Something was suspicious about him, but my people would certainly find out sooner or later. Unlike my fake ass boogie cousin, I was in the streets. A nigga could tell her anything, and her dumb ass would believe it.

"I don't know what you're talking about," he said, afraid this was a set up.

"Baby," I said, stroking his arm, "my cousin is family, but I want to talk business with you outside of here." He listened intensely. "After the club, meet me at The Hilton on Wake Forest Road. Room 125. Me and my bitch are staying there tonight."

He never agreed, just said that he'd think about it, and I understood. He didn't know me, and thought this may have seemed strange. I'd heard about bitches luring niggas to hotels and having them robbed or shot. Brooklyn was smarter than I thought.

The world famous DJ Deluxe called last call at the bar. The club was almost over and we headed back to the hotel. Shortly after we entered our suite, there was a knock on the door.

"You expecting somebody?" Joy asked, walking

toward the door.

"My homeboy, Brooklyn, is coming through. I need to talk to him about some business," I said, knowing it was him. His curiosity for two fine bitches with big asses in one room got the best of him, and I knew he'd show up. *Let's see if he's really all about Oshyn*, I thought.

"Who is it?" Joy asked, through the door.

He stood at the door defiantly, and refused to say a word. I told her to let him in and she followed my orders. He walked in with a grim look on his face and his heat by his side.

"Put that shit up, it ain't even like that," I said, convincing him this wasn't a stick up. "Joy, can you excuse us for a second? This won't take long."

She gathered her shit together, went to the bathroom and started running our bath water. "That's a bad bitch, isn't she?" I said to Brooklyn.

"She alright," he said, watching Joy's juicy-ass walk away.

"Oh, so you're not into fine women?"

"Yeah, but only Oshyn."

That comment ate me alive. *Why was Oshyn always the one to get the best of everything? We'll see how long he stays faithful, I thought. I know how to changes minds. Pussy is a deadly thing.*

"I heard that you're doing big things down in this country town," I blurted out. "You getting money, and I want in."

"How do you...does Oshyn know?" he asked, afraid that Oshyn had found out about his double life.

"Nah, she ain't in the streets. I am. The streets talk and I listen. But don't worry, your secret is safe with me," I said, running my French manicured fingers down his face and into his mouth. He turned away quickly and pushed me from in front of him. "I need you to do something else for me," I said, trying to reel him back in. "I need you to clean up some money for me."

"I'm not an errand boy, clean up your own fucking money," he said, as he headed for the door.

"I have a million dollars that I need accounted for and you have the businesses I need to recycle it with." He stopped in his tracks and turned back around. I knew that would get his attention. "I'll give you ten percent for your troubles."

"A million dollars? How the fuck you get that kind of money?" he asked confused.

"What can I say, the pussy business is great and well worth what I get paid for it," I said, winking at him.

"Why me? You don't know me. Why don't you just ask your cousin?"

"Because we don't get along, she likes to judge. And more importantly, I figured you could get me some properties much easier than I could. I can see us having a great business relationship. With the perfect story and all the paper in the world to back it up, my portfolio will be clean in no time. Not to mention the hundred grand

I'm breaking you off with." I knew I had him. If my pussy wouldn't lure him in, I knew my money would.

"I'll clean this money up for you, but don't tell Oshyn nothing about this."

"Yeah, yeah, yeah, whatever," I said, rolling my eyes at him. I didn't take to kindly to threats, especially ones involving Oshyn and her feelings.

He took his hand and wrapped it around my throat, cutting off my air. My eyes got wide as I gasped for whatever breath I could and tried to pry his hands off my neck. This was something that I hadn't expected.

"I said, I'll clean this money up for you and you're *NOT* going to tell Oshyn anything about it," he repeated. "Do you understand me?"

It seemed like his grip got tighter as I struggled to muster out the word, "Yes." He let go and I fell to the floor, gagging from my lack of oxygen. He straightened up his clothes and walked out the door.

*Damn, there's something about him we obviously don't know about*, I thought. *Oshyn, better watch out.*

# 11

# CHLOE

I sat on the porch and watched Beef wash his white BMW 745. It was a nice day, about sixty degrees. It wasn't too cold, but a bit breezy. We definitely needed the break from the heat, and I was grateful for the rain that cooled things down.

"Babe, hand me the wax," Beef said, pointing at the yellow bottle sitting on the driveway.

"My nails are wet nigga, get it yourself," I said, blowing on my freshly polished nails.

"GET YOUR LAZY ASS UP AND HAND ME THE FUCKING BOTTLE!" he shouted.

Beef was obviously sick of my shit. I got up and handed it to him with a smile on my face. I liked it when he talked rough.

Beef was sexy, and his two hundred and fifty pound frame put me in the mind of a football player. When I first met him at the gym, I thought he was a defensive tackle for some NFL team, but quickly learned he was a big time drug-dealer, originally from Chicago.

He tried to treat me nice, but I was a bitch. I had to be because I couldn't allow him or anyone else to get too close. All niggas were the same and deserved to be treated like shit. But I would make an exception for Brooklyn, if he'd stop acting so stupid. Beef's dick was entirely too small for his size, but his money was long. That was a great substitute. I ended up popping myself off after we fucked, because he definitely couldn't do the job. Or whenever Joy came through, she made us both cum. His nasty ass loved that shit.

I didn't know much about Beef, but I knew he had moved to North Carolina with his aunt a couple of years ago. Apparently his mother had died of a drug overdose, leaving her sister to take care of him. Me and Beef had only known each other for two weeks, and I was already staying at his crib. I guess you could say I had a great case of pussy power. Beef said that he wanted to take care of me, and that I would never have to work again. Too bad he didn't know the truth — that I was only here temporarily until I could get things straightened. I couldn't complain though, the crib was banging. He had great taste.

"Baby, I'm hungry, what you cooking today?" he asked.

"I'm not cooking shit, and I'm hungry too, so you need to pick up something when you go out!"

"Lazy bitch! You lucky your pussy is good," he said, reminding himself why he put up with my shit.

*If I could only get Brooklyn to say that*, I thought.

I had been watching Brooklyn for some time now, studying him. He was the one I wanted, and would to do anything to get him. I didn't know why he stepped to Oshyn anyway. Her body was obviously not better than mine. She always got the good ones.

I fucked with a lot of men, but Brooklyn was perfect. He had hustle money, clean money, and was very well dressed. He never wore clothes that hung off his body. His style was Euro.

He was well educated. Hood when he had to be, but remained professional most of the time. He took very good care of himself, and I liked that.

I often wondered where in life did things go wrong for me. Why was my life so fucked up? It always seemed like Oshyn got the luxuries and I got everyone's ass to kiss. Grandma always treated her better and seemed to love her more. None of it ever made any since.

I remember my grandmother praying for me at night while I pretended to be asleep soon after my mother died. She'd pray night after night that my mother's evil spirit wouldn't enter my body, and I began to hate her for that. I loved my mother. How dare she pray for my mother's spirit not to enter my body? My mother wasn't evil. She did what we do best.

Oshyn's mother, Aunt Roslyn, wrote Grandma from

jail all the time. I guess she stopped writing me after she figured that I would never respond. I didn't want to reconcile with her. She had the rest of her life to think about what she had done to my mother.

I thought about the last letter she wrote me, that I had memorized word for word. I even kept it in my purse at all times, hoping that one day it would make sense. I grabbed my purse off the porch and took out the familiar piece of paper.

*My sweet, sweet Chloe,*

*No words can express the pain I feel for what has happened. I know that you hate me, but one day when you're all grown up, I hope you'll let me explain everything to you. I never wanted to hurt you, honestly I didn't. But I have made my peace with God and ask for your forgiveness. Please write me back soon, and if you choose not to remember that night, always remember, I love you.*
*Aunt Roslyn*

Maybe she finally realized that I just couldn't forgive her, because the letters stop coming after that. I was still on the porch fanning my nails when Beef called me again. Quickly, I stuffed the letter back in my purse and stood up on the porch.

"Baby…"

"What?" I screamed, irritated that he always called me baby, and never Chloe. We weren't that cool to be using pet names.

"You better watch who the fuck you talking to, yo!" he snapped.

"I'm sorry, baby, I just got a lot on my mind. I didn't mean to snap," I said, not wanting to get him too upset.

"I'm hungry," he repeated.

"Alright."

I headed in the house to fix his punk ass some food. An hour later, I had a nice little meal waiting for him.

"Is this it?" he asked, looking at the chicken and rice on the plate.

"Yeah, everything else is frozen and will take a minute to thaw out. This should hold you for now."

"Thank you," he said, not wanting to argue.

I stared at him as he ate the food like a starving child. At that moment, he was really becoming a turn off. Five minutes later his plate was clean, and he had the nerve to hand me the dirty plate.

"I'm getting ready to go to work," he said.

When we first met, Beef told me that he worked in construction. It only took me two days of asking around on the streets to find out that he didn't. I liked that he tried to hide his illegal doings from me. He wanted to protect me, just in case something went down. No one else ever gave a fuck.

"When you coming home?" I asked, pretending to

care as I walked to the sink.

"A couple of hours. I'm just going to collect some loot. Why? You wanna do something later?"

"Maybe."

"Bet. I'll call you before I head in."

He gave me a kiss on the cheek and walked out the door. I decided to call Oshyn and see what she was doing.

"Hey, Oshyn, what you up to?"

"Nothing. Brooklyn, Apples and I are watching movies. What's up with you?"

"Oh…and I wasn't invited? What's up with that?" I asked, unable to hide my anger.

"It was spur of the moment, nothing planned. You can still come through if you want. The movie is almost over though."

"I'm on my way."

CLICK

I was heated. There was no way this family shit was going down, and I wasn't invited. And Apples. Apples always came before me, Oshyn's own flesh and blood. I hated that bitch. She came between everything. I got dressed and made my way to North Raleigh in record time. Using my spare key Oshyn had given me, I let myself in.

"Hey, y'all!"

"What's up," everyone said, in unison.

Their eyes were glued to *The Texas Chainsaw*

*Massacre* that was on the projection screen in Oshyn's movie room. No one moved. No one even cared that I was there.

I helped myself to a seat next to Apples. She rolled her eyes. The feelings were mutual.

"What time did this…"

"SHHH!!!" everyone said.

"Fuck y'all too!"

"Hey, Brooklyn," I said, hoping he would notice my cleavage through my low cut wife beater. Hopefully he'd loosen the guerilla grip on Oshyn.

The head nod. That's what he hit me with. The infamous head nod.

The '*you don't mean shit, don't talk to me right now, play your position*' head nod. That's all I got.

Oshyn looked at me, trying to read my expression. She seemed suspicious and had a right to be. I wanted that nigga bad.

When the movie ended, that stupid bitch, Apples, jumped up like she couldn't wait to get away from me.

"All right, Oshyn, I'm out," Apples said. "I'm tired."

"Alright, sweetheart, see you in the morning. Love you."

"Love you too. Bye, Brooklyn…Chloe."

I hit her with the head nod. The international symbol for 'Fuck You'.

Apples put her middle finger up as she headed out the door. I blew her ass a kiss and turned my attention to

Oshyn and Brooklyn.

"What are you doing for the rest of the night?" Oshyn asked, still hugged up on her new boyfriend.

"Nothing. Beef is working so I figured I'd chill here for a while."

"Not tonight," she said, while he massaged her feet. Brooklyn never looked my way. It was if I was invisible to him. Maybe I was. "I need a little privacy tonight," Oshyn said, never taking her eyes off Brooklyn.

"Whatever," I said, rolling my eyes as I grabbed my purse.

*I can't believe this. Every man I want, I always get, but with Brooklyn, I'ma nobody,* I thought.

"Alright, I'm gone," I said.

They hit me with the peace sign. Not even a good bye.

I let myself out.

❀ ❀ ❀

*BREAKFAST AT TIFFANY'S* was an upscale breakfast spot in North Hills. The food was banging. Not worth the price, but Beef was paying.

"What did you do after I left last night?" he asked, while stuffing the steak and cheese omelet down his throat.

"I went to Oshyn's house and watched movies with her, Brooklyn and Apples."

"Word. Oshyn and that nigga still kicking it like that? They been chillin' for a minute…like a couple of months now. I don't know the nigga that well, but we're in the same line of work, so I do know he don't keep bitches that long. Oshyn must be a good catch. That's what's up. They seem happy."

"Whatever nigga! You need to worry about what seems happier over here, a'ight," I snapped.

"Shut the fuck up, Chloe, with your hating ass. Be happy for somebody for once in your life. Everybody ain't out to hurt you," Beef said.

But that was the thing. Everyone *was* out to hurt me, and I was convinced. Everyone owed me for my pain and suffering, especially Oshyn.

"Can I get the check, please?" Beef asked, ready to go.

"Yes, sir, right away," the waiter said, hurrying off.

We continued to talk about nothing, when I looked up and saw two familiar people.

"Is that Brooklyn and Apples?" I said, needing conformation.

Now I knew that I wasn't shit, but Apples, I would've never thought. Not in a million years.

"Yeah, that's them," Beef said, trying to figure out my intentions.

We watched as the hostess seated them at a table in the back of the restaurant.

"Chloe, mind your business," Beef said, as I stood up.

"This is my business," I said, heading toward their

table.

Beef tried to stop me by pulling my arm, but I was able to jerk away. I guess he decided to follow me, just in case some shit kicked off.

The closer I got, the more I noticed the bags from all the expensive stores. From the looks of things, he'd taken her on a shopping spree. Hermes, Gucci, Jimmy Choo, and most importantly, an aqua bag with the name Tiffany & Co. on it.

"What the fuck is this?" I asked, barging in front of the table.

"It's a restaurant, and can you please lower your tone?" Brooklyn's fine ass said, not intimidated at all by my presence. He looked at Beef for a moment, wondering why he allowed me to cause a scene.

"No, fuck that shit," I said, a little louder. "You're my cousin's best friend and you fucking her nigga?" I asked Apples.

"Chloe, shut the fuck up. Ain't nobody doing shit. You're always trying to start something," Apples said, with a serious attitude.

Apples was a fighter. We all were. I knew at any minute she was going to get up and swing. She had a low tolerance level for bullshit.

"You shut the fuck up, bitch!" I snapped back.

"Why don't your miserable ass go and kill yourself? You're no good to anybody. Go ahead and put yourself out of your misery," Apples said, waiting on my next move.

I paused and then said, "I asked Quon the last time we spoke why didn't he just kill you!"

Everything froze. Brooklyn and Beef didn't know what had happened, but they both sensed a war getting ready to go down.

Apples picked up the steak knife on the table and stood up. Our eyes never left each other.

Before things got completely out of hand, Brooklyn grabbed Apples and Beef pulled me away.

"Ladies, that's enough!" Brooklyn said.

We were loud and had created a scene, but I had accomplished everything I wanted. Even though I didn't want Apples to know that I was fucking her baby father, Quon, from time to time, the sheer look of horror in her eyes was well worth the beans being spilled.

She was terrified of that man, and had every right to be. Everybody in Rochester was afraid of him. He took a life as often as he put on his shoes. He had nothing to lose. Quon was a good nigga, when he wasn't high on dope. He picked up the habit after Apples left him and moved to Raleigh. It's funny how, after all the niggas he killed, the thing that took him over the edge was pussy.

He went flat out crazy and has been looking for Apples and Bella ever since. If he wasn't so high, he may have found her by now.

After convincing Beef that I was calm, he let me go. I took a few steps away and turned around to take a picture of the two lovebirds with my picture phone. This was my way to finally get Apples out of the picture.

"Give me that phone," Beef said, trying to grab it with his strong arms.

"Hell no, I'm showing this to Oshyn."

"Why don't you just mind your business, this don't have shit to do with you," he ordered.

I ignored his comment, while thinking of the bigger picture.

I didn't care what Beef thought about me, because he was temporary.

❀   ❀   ❀

"Hey, Oshyn. What you up to?" I asked, anxious to tell her the news. I had called Oshyn as soon as Beef dropped me off at his house to take care of some business.

"Nothing," she answered. "Washing clothes and waiting for Booklyn to get here. We're supposed to be going out for lunch."

"Well, I'm coming through. It's something important that I need to talk to you about."

"Is everything okay?" she asked, worried.

"I'm on the way," I said, not answering her question.

I parked my car in front of her house and held my arms open while Micah ran up to me. I loved him so much. He was the only person who didn't judge me and was so innocent and pure.

"Where's Mommy?" I asked. He pointed to the house. "You playing by yourself?"

"No, I'm playing hide and seek with Bella. She's hiding."

"Okay, Stank. Don't run into the street."

"Okay!" Micah said, hurrying back to find his friend.

"Hey, Oshyn!" I said, greeted by the sounds of The O'Jays as I walked into the house. That was cleaning music. The same music we grew up on with our mothers.

She still saw hers.

I missed mine.

"Hey, Chloe," Oshyn said. "What happened? Are you okay?"

"Yeah, but I need to holla at you about something."

She lowered the music as we took a seat on the couch.

"Where's Apples?" I asked, wondering what excuse she gave Oshyn for watching Bella.

"She has a class on Saturday mornings. She should be back soon," Oshyn said, checking her watch.

"Honey, I hate to tell you this, but me and Beef just left North Hills, and I saw Apples and Brooklyn eating breakfast together. They been shopping and everything. Must've had a long night. A good one too…"

Silence.

Dead Silence.

"Oshyn, did you hear me?" I asked, lightly touching

her arm.

"Yeah, I heard you," she said, pulling away. "Apples is my best friend, she wouldn't do anything like that to me."

Oshyn was positive that I had received the wrong info.

"I knew you weren't going to believe me, so I took pictures on my phone for proof."

I showed her the flicks and she studied them carefully. She turned the camera in several different directions, trying to convince herself it wasn't them.

"This can't be right," she said to herself.

"Where did Brooklyn say he was?" I asked, trying to help build my case.

"Brooklyn said he had to take care of some business. And why would Apples lie to me about being in school? What's going on?" she asked, with a confused expression on her face.

My job was done.

With Apples out of the way, Oshyn would start spending more time with me, and Brooklyn was sure to be cut out the picture.

*Now he's all mine*, I thought, as I rubbed Oshyn's back with a devilish grin.

I sat with her as she cried.

# 12

# OSHYN

I wanted to wake up from my nightmare. *This couldn't be happening*, I thought, as I tried to piece together all the deceitful information. Apples was my sister, my best friend, and I loved her. There had to be an explanation. There was something about this that just didn't add up.

I gave Brooklyn my heart, and was now starting to regret it. The saddest thing about it all was that I loved him. I fell in love from the start, and played hard to get as long as I could.

I sat on my couch and cried. I cried so hard that my stomach cramped, cried so hard that I couldn't breathe. I expected Apples to come to me and say that she had seen Brooklyn and they had grabbed a quick bite to eat. I needed her to say something that would make me feel better.

"That isn't reality," I mumbled, hitting myself in the

head.

Micah and Bella came inside to grab a cup of water from the kitchen. I insisted they do that once every hour. I wanted them to stay hydrated.

"Mommy, what's wrong?" my son asked as he followed me, hearing my slight sniffles. Bella looked confused, and followed closely behind too.

"Nothing, baby. Mommy's heart hurts. It hurts bad." I clenched the chenille throw pillow as close to my stomach as I could, trying to suffocate the pain.

Micah put his little arms around my waist and held me as tightly as he could. "Don't cry, Mommy," he said softly.

Bella joined in the bear hug. I looked at them both intensely, and prayed they turned out to be best friends like Apples and I. Children are so sweet. Their innocence speaks volumes of their character. I wish I could shelter them from this world and all the pain that they'll experience; the broken hearts, the unforgiveness.

I was sick and tired of always being hurt.

I cried in my son's arms, embarrassed that he was my comforter, but glad he was there.

I quickly tried to dry my eyes as I heard the front door open. It was obvious that I was making a fool of myself in front of Micah, but no one else needed to see me like this.

"Oshyn, I'm here," Apples said, entering the room cheerfully. "Sorry it took so long, but I had to stay a little later to talk with my professor. Girl, he's cute!"

*Lies. Straight lies,* I thought. I wondered, for the first time, how many she had told before. She did it so easily, so flawlessly, so effortlessly. She even looked me straight in the eyes.

"What's wrong, Oshyn?" she asked, noticing the tears streaming down my face.

"Mommy's heart hurts," Micah said, still holding me tightly.

"Micah and Bella, go back outside and play. Apples and I have to talk."

They reluctantly obliged and trotted back outside, instantly forgetting my pain.

"Oshyn, what's wrong?" Apples asked again, this time taking a seat next to me.

I flipped my phone open and pulled up the picture that Chloe had instantly e-mailed to me. Without saying a word, I handed her the phone, showing the evidence.

"O…, it's not what you…"

WHOP!!

I banged her in the head with my fist, and followed that with two more punches in the face before I calmed down. She just sat there, stunned. She never moved. She simply held her jaw and sat there.

"Why Apples?" I asked crying. "I love you. I would do anything for you, why would you do this to me?"

"Oshyn, it's not what you think!"

"Shut up!! You lied and told me you were in school.

And I guess you're the business that Brooklyn said he had to take care of today. You betrayed me. I expected Chloe, but never you."

I remember when my grandmother use to warn me about bringing close friends around my man. I use to always listen to her horror stories about the friends she trusted the most, and how her boyfriend ended up in the friend's bed. I took pride knowing that none of my friends would do that to me, but I guess I'm no different. I lived by a code of honor that apparently everyone else has forgotten.

"Give me my house key back, and get the fuck out my house!"

"He's proposing to you!" Apples shouted, with tears running down her bruised face. "He was talking to a pastor about his decision, and he asked me not to go to class so that he could show me the ring that he bought you for the surprise engagement party tonight."

Apples got up and walked toward the door, where the shopping bags were. I hadn't noticed the names earlier, Hermes, Gucci and Jimmy Choo. She whipped out a beautiful red dress and held it up high.

"I was supposed to make you put this on and invite you to dinner later on to celebrate your accomplishments at the office."

I was stunned, embarrassed and most of all, sorry. I hadn't given her any credit. She had never done anything to hurt me before. I shook my head with frustration. I couldn't believe I'd listened to the one person who I trusted the least. I walked over to Apples and held her tightly.

"I'm so sorry Apples…I'm so sorry."

"It's okay," she said, more hurt than I thought. "I guess there's a limit to how much trust you have in me."

"No…no…no… That's not true. You're my most trusted friend. I just made a big mistake." We held each other tightly, sharing each other's pain.

"Mommy, your heart hurts too?" Bella asked, walking back in. We never heard them come in.

"No, sweetheart, not anymore. Everything is going to be okay," Apples said, looking at me.

I knew that meant she'd forgiven me.

"So, lady, tonight is your special night," Apples said, giving me a pat on the back.

She tried to ease the tension between us, so that my night wouldn't be ruined. But I was no fool, she was still a bit upset.

"He wants to marry me for real?" I asked, with a wide grin.

"Yes, he does," she responded, with a smile.

I screamed and jumped on the couch to do a fancy dance.

"Oh, my God. I finally got my Prince! By the way, is the ring big?" I blurted out.

We both laughed.

❋  ❋  ❋

Hours later, we headed out of the door. The stars were extremely bright outside. They resembled spotlights, pointing all in my direction. Maybe it was the universe telling me that this was right.

Brooklyn had the Bentley Continental GT waiting outside my house at exactly 8:30. I asked Apples if it was a rental, but she had flipped back into a sour mood. We rode to the party in silence, not having really much to say. She was still visibly bothered from my accusations earlier, and my apology obviously wasn't enough.

"Apples, I'm really sorry about earlier," I said sincerely. "You know it's been a long time since I've been in a relationship. Insecurity has really been an issue since the whole Trent ordeal, but I'll do better. I promise."

"It's okay, really," she said, with a slight smile. "I can only imagine what it must've looked like. I guess I might've thought the same way had the tables been turned." She paused in the plush cream leather seats and gazed out the window. "Nah, I take that back. I would've trusted you more. I would've let you explain." Her voice got deeper and louder. "I would've at least given you that chance."

She was right, and I couldn't say anything. I knew I'd have to spend some time making things up to her, but whatever it took, I would do it. I almost lost a great friendship and all of this because of Chloe. Her intentions were never good.

"Were almost here," Apples said, as we approached the 'secret location'. I reclined back in the seat, rubbing my temples. I was excited about my future, hoping to erase the past. I had no doubt, though, that Apples and I would reconcile our problems. Our love was unconditional.

"Hey, Oshyn?"

"Yeah?"

"Chloe mentioned something about talking to Quon?" Apples asked, out of the blue.

"When?" I asked, hearing the fear in her voice.

"When me and Brooklyn were at breakfast this morning. I told her to kill herself, and she responded by saying she'd asked Quon why he didn't just kill me when he had the chance."

I laughed.

"Why are you laughing?" she asked, in a serious tone.

"I just imagined you telling Chloe to kill herself. I would've given anything to hear that."

"Oh."

"Girl, cheer up! She was probably just bullshitting you. You told the bitch to kill herself. She had to come back at you with something hard. Chloe knows that nothing else scares you except Quon, so that is what she used."

"I hope so. If that nigga knew where I lived…Oshyn, he'll kill me and Bella," she said, letting the tears flow down her lightly freckled face. I wiped them away while she looked out of the window.

"Don't cry, babe. Look, I know you and Chloe don't really fuck with each other, but she wouldn't do anything like that. She knows that Quon is a cold killer, and he has nothing to lose. She wouldn't…" I paused. I thought about all the things I thought Chloe would never do, and realized she'd done them all. Chills went up my spine, and my confident attitude changed. "I'll ask her. But don't worry about anything. You know she's just a hater."

"Sure," Apples said, still visibly upset. She looked out the window before speaking, as if she'd gotten some sort of cue. "We're here!" she shouted, trying to get in a festive mood.

The driver pulled into the parking lot of a million dollar custom estate. The sign read Wakefield Plantation. The red carpet was rolled out from my car door to the gigantic home, and people posed as the paparazzi beside the car flashing a million pictures.

"He put a lot of thought and preparation into this. I really wish that we could've kept this a secret," Apples remarked.

"Yeah, me too!"

We hugged, ignoring the flashing lights.

"Congratulations," she said, wiping the tears from her face.

"Thank you! Let's go!"

The driver walked around and opened my door. The fragrant blend of Eskimo white rose petals flooded the red carpet. On cue, someone released what looked to be about twenty doves out of a cage, and I watched with a grin as they flew into the star filled sky. We walked the red carpet, feeling like a star.

Two tall men, dressed in white butler suits, opened the fourteen-carat gold-rimmed French doors simultaneously, that led us to the back yard. The amazing landscaping display of blended flowers surrounded us with its sweet damp fragrance, and its soothing waterfall. The twenty-foot long, heart shaped in-ground pool had votive candles and red rose petals floating on the crystal blue waters. The ambient lighting complimented the full moon and showered us with an instant peace of mind.

*Wow*, I thought, *my baby had outdone himself.* I felt so blessed to be the woman who snagged Brooklyn Jones. I was glad I had a heads up about the proposal ahead of time, otherwise, I would've passed out after seeing all of this.

Just when I thought I'd seen it all, I almost shitted on myself when I saw the faces of everyone I loved most in my life. There were at least three hundred people in attendance, all dressed in black. I made my way across the yard and greeted my guests. I ran into old friends from Rochester, people I hadn't seen in years.

I looked around and noticed Chloe was nowhere in

sight. I secretly hoped that she wouldn't even come. I hated that I felt that way, but then wondered if Brooklyn had even invited her.

Although a black tie affair, everyone was dressed appropriately, except for me. Brooklyn obviously wanted me to stand out when he picked out my red satin, off the shoulder Valentino dress. I practically floated across the room in my gold Guiseppe sandals, covered in shimmering crystals. He made sure I was the main attraction, and everyone confirmed it with the steady stream of compliments that kept rolling in. Hell, I felt like Julia Roberts in the movie *Pretty Woman.*

"Congratulations, boss lady!" Brian said, catching my attention. My eyes focused on the big boob, blonde girl glued to his arm.

"Thanks, crazy," I said, kissing him on the cheek.

"This is my girl, Cherish. Cherish, this is my boss lady and friend, Oshyn."

"It's a pleasure," I replied, rolling my eyes at Brian as we hugged. He knew exactly what I meant.

I wanted him to settle down and find a wife. I was sick of seeing him with a different bitch every other week. I wouldn't have cared if it was anyone else, but I considered him a friend.

The music played, the guest drank and danced, and I said a silent prayer to God, thanking Him for my fast growing company, my family, and the times when I could have lost my mind. Most of all, I thanked Him for sending me Brooklyn.

In all the excitement, I realized that I hadn't seen the reason all of this existed, my man. *I hope he has no more surprises, I can't handle it,* I thought, as I turned around smelling a familiar scent. There before me, stood my knight and shining armor. His aura demanded attention, covered in Dolce and Gabbana from head to toe, all black, of course. His smile sent chills down my back, along with his moist lips that gently pressed against mine. Damn, he smelled soooooooo…good.

"Hey, baby," he whispered, "you look beautiful." He grabbed my hand and said, "Come with me, I want you to meet somebody."

I looked her up and down, wondering who she was. Her shoulder length weave was platinum blonde and her black suit, rimmed with gold trim was hot, along with the gold Petit Paton stilettos she wore. You could tell she was older, but she refused to dress accordingly.

"Ma, this is Oshyn. Oshyn, this is my mother, Tracy," he said, hoping we'd bond.

"Hey, daughter-in-law," she said, in a squeaky high-pitched New York accent. "She's so pretty, Brooklyn, good job," she added, while she examined me as if I wasn't there. "My son has told me a lot about you. He has never introduced me to any woman, much less considered marriage. You must be really special."

"Thank you, Ms. Trac…"

"Ma! You call me, Ma!" she insisted.

"Thank you, Ma," I continued. "It was so nice meeting you." We embraced and kept it moving.

"I can't believe you'd do all of this for me! Whose house is this anyway? When did you have time to put all this together? How much did this…"

"SSShhhhhh," he said, sticking his index finger to my colored lips. "All of that doesn't matter. What matters is that this is our day and that you're happy."

I love him. Truly I do. Water welled up in my eyes at the thought of me finally finding my soul mate. A man who truly loves me the way I deserve to be loved. A man, who cherishes the thought of spending the rest of his life with me. My future, my husband.

"Apples told me what happened earlier," he said, looking into my eyes. "I hated that the surprise was ruined, but with the look on your face, it was still worth it. For the record, I would never do anything like that to betray your trust. I love you. Since the day we first met, you fascinated me, intrigued me. And Apples…that girl is loyal to you. She would die before she did anything to hurt you."

"Yeah, I know," I said, holding my head down. "I feel so bad about the whole thing," I said, recalling the events from earlier today.

"We'll make it up to her," he said, as he lifted my head back up. "Feel bad tomorrow, but not tonight. You're going to have fun tonight."

He dragged me out to the dance floor, and we danced

like we were in the middle of a fairytale.

"They're so in love," I heard a couple mumble from the side of the dance floor.

"Baby, where's Chloe?" I asked, now realizing that she definitely wasn't at the party.

"Fuck Chloe!" he barked.

There was my answer. So, I left it alone.

Micah ran from out the crowd and hugged me. "Moommmiieeee!" he said, excited that he'd finally found me.

"Hey, Stank, where you been?" I asked, hugging him tightly. He looked so handsome in his suit. I hated that he reminded me of his father.

"I asked Micah for your hand in marriage before I planned any of this. He was with it," Brooklyn bragged.

Micah stood there with a smile just as wide as mine, proving that my dimples ran in the family.

"He said he's going to be my new daddy!" Micah shouted. He seemed excited about having Brooklyn around permanently. He would be the first male figure to ever be a part of his life.

I told Micah that his real father died. I wasn't sure whether or not it was true. Someone said Trent had been shot a year or so ago, but I never called back home to find out. I wasn't even sad when I heard the news, because he'd always been dead to us. But this time, Micah was getting a real daddy.

Brooklyn led Micah and I to the stage and led me to

the huge chair, which was my throne for the night. Our guest, which seemed to have grown, hovered around the platform. The piano soloist played a soft ballad to set the mood for the speech.

The sky was dark on this November night, and the stars were magnificent. It was about sixty degrees with no breeze, which made it easy for the guest who were given candles to hold up. Brooklyn grabbed the mic, looked me in the eyes and began:

"Oshyn, you are the definition of a woman. You amaze me, you inspire me, and you make me whole. Your smile, your kindness, your patience, your virtue…your love…I've got to have. Since the day we met, I couldn't imagine spending a second without you in my life. I honor you and *our* son. I want to be the man that makes your heart smile. The man that makes all your worries go away. It would give me great pleasure to be able to call myself your husband."

I cried big crocodile tears. Everyone else was too. Brooklyn got down on one knee and opened the velvet box. Inside laid a flawless nine-carat emerald cut diamond ring. My damp hands trembled as he put our new symbol of commitment on my ring finger.

"Yes, baby, I would love to be your wife!"

The crowd roared with excitement as Brooklyn lifted me up and embraced me tightly. The crowd cheered and simultaneously bottles were heard popping everywhere.

Brooklyn grabbed my hand and led me to the front

of the gigantic house. He stopped for a moment and winked at Micah. *What did the two of them have up their sleeves,* I wondered? My eyes got big and my mouth opened wide as I stared at the hot air balloon that read: BROOKLYN'S OSHYN.

"What if I would've said no?" I asked jokingly.

"Yeah, right," he said, as he led me to the hot air balloon. The crowd waved goodbye as the balloon lifted us off in the calm night sky. I'm sure they were all ready to get back to the party of the year, and I was ready to get to my man.

"You know how to drive this thing?" I asked, thinking there should've been someone else inside with us.

"I got an operating license, just so that it would be me and you alone."

He came closer and lifted me out of my dress. I stood in front of him in my laced red La Perla set. He licked his lips like he was starving at a Thanksgiving feast. I guess in a way, I was too. He held me tight, pressing his firm dick against my stomach. He was so tall and fit, I felt protected. He licked my body from top to bottom, devouring my pussy. His foreplay was amazing. We made love for the first time above the city for the rest of the night, consummating our union, before we even officially tied the night.

# 13

# CHLOE

"Girl, the party was bananas! The mansion was something straight off of MTV cribs. The shit was crazy!" The loud mouth girl sitting beside me had been talking non-stop, and I was ready to go.

Even though I stayed in the salon twice a week, I hated getting my hair done. My hair was too long, which always meant extra time under the dryer. Keke always took her time rolling my hair, so I had no choice but to listen to the loud bitch sitting next to me on her cell phone.

"Everybody had on black except for his girl. That bitch had a bad red dress on. I told your dumb ass to come, there were a lot of niggas, a whole different breed. These muthafuckas must've been from up North, because I've never seen them around before. And girl, Brooklyn and that bitch...I think her name was Oshyn, flew away in a hot air balloon."

Brooklyn? Oshyn? I couldn't be hearing right. Suddenly my ears turned into antennas, and I wanted every detail of whatever it was loud mouth was talking about.

"Are you talking about that big ass engagement party last night?" another hairstylist asked.

"Yeah," the loud one said, now carrying on two conversations. "The shit was so romantic, straight out of the movies."

"I heard that her ring was big as hell!" the hairstylist said, using her hands to describe the ring.

"Hell, yeah. It was big as shit! At least ten carats," loud mouth stated.

"You said his name was Brooklyn and hers, Oshyn," I said, not being able to take the torture any longer. I had to know what this chick was talking about. There weren't too many people named Brooklyn and Oshyn in the world, and it couldn't have been a coincidence that she was talking about them in the same conversation.

"Yeah, I believe her name was Oshyn, because my boyfriend is one of Brooklyn's homeboys. He said that she owned a real estate company."

My suspicions were confirmed. I got antsy and couldn't sit still. My stomach started to hurt.

"You said they got engaged?" I asked.

"Oh, my God, yes! Honey, it was the party of the year! There were about five hundred people there, and I don't think there was a dry eye in the building. Even my punk ass boyfriend got teary eyed. It was some special shit."

"Chloe, isn't your cousin named Oshyn?" Keke asked.

"Yes, Keke. Do you need to know my social security number too?" I shouted.

"Damn, Chloe, what the fuck is your problem?" Keke snapped back.

I ignored her because I wasn't in the mood to go back and forth. I also gave the loud mouth bitch a cold stare that said don't even fucking ask. I was furious and embarrassed. My first cousin had gotten engaged, and I wasn't there. I had to find out about this 'mega party' from some bum bitch in the hair salon. Oshyn had pulled some foul shit. I took some money out of my Fendi Spy bag, and hit Keke off with her money.

"I gotta go," I said, as I got up to get my things together. "I need to take care of some shit that just came up."

"But, Chloe, your hair is soaking wet," Keke said, mad that she had spent her time rolling it up.

"It's not like I didn't pay your ass. I'll be back tomorrow to get it done again, a'ight?" I was out the door with a head full of rollers before she gave me an answer. I had to get down to the bottom of this shit immediately.

Thank goodness traffic was light, because I rode down New Bern Avenue doing way over the speed limit.

I drove straight to Oshyn's office, and caught Brian just as he was getting out of his convertible Jag. He was on his way in the building when I yelled his name.

"Brian!" I said, trying to slow him down.

"Hey, Chloe," he said, walking toward my car. "What's up with the hair?" he continued, touching the gray rollers that covered my head. He had never seen me like this. Actually, no one had.

"Fuck that," I snapped, moving my head from his curious fingers. "Where's Oshyn?" I asked, not ready to teach black hair 101 to the fine ass white boy. Brian might have had a chance with me, but I had ran the numbers, and he just didn't make enough.

"Oh, she'll be right back. She had to run to the bank. Hey, why didn't I see you at the party last night? Only a crackhead would've missed that party!"

I wanted to spit in his face. I wasn't in the mood for jokes, even though I knew he wasn't playing. He genuinely wanted to know why Oshyn's only cousin wasn't by her side while she got engaged. That was a question I needed answers to myself.

Before I could give him a bullshit answer, Oshyn pulled up in a sparkling new black Aston Martin Vanquish S. The system was blaring so loud she didn't even notice I was there.

"Gift from Brooklyn!" Brian shouted, confirming what I had already knew. "This shit is HOT!" he added, drooling.

"OSHYN!" I screamed, trying to get her attention. I had heard enough. "OSHYN!" I repeated, as I ran over to the black beauty, realizing that she still hadn't noticed my presence. I banged on the glass until she rolled the window down.

"Hey, what's up, cousin?" she said, with a big smile on her face. "Look what Brooklyn got me!"

"Yeah, whatever. I need to holla at you now!" I demanded.

"Well, can it wait because I have a meeting to get to? And why do you have those big ass rollers in your hair?"

"Look, I need to holla at you NOW!" I repeated, this time with a bit more authority in my voice.

"Calm down!" she said, looking at me like I was crazy. She got out the car, and pressed the key to activate the alarm. "Brain, can you go and get all the paperwork together? I need a few minutes to talk with Chloe."

"Sure, honey" Brian said, as he walked in the building.

I finally had her undivided attention.

"Okay, make it quick," Oshyn said, obviously rushing me.

"What's this I heard about you getting engaged? I'm your fucking cousin, and I'm hearing through the streets about a party you had at a mansion last night?"

"Chloe, Chloe, Chloe," she said, trying to calm me down. "Yes, Brooklyn and I did get engaged last night, but it wasn't my fault that you weren't there. I didn't even know about the party myself. I meant to call you today, but I've been so busy at work."

"Save that shit for somebody else, and stop feeding me the bullshit!" I screamed, rolling my eyes.

"Shut the fuck up and listen sometimes, damn!" Oshyn said. "When you saw Apples and Brooklyn at breakfast yesterday, they weren't creeping. They were planning our engagement party that I had no clue about. I can't invite you to something that I knew nothing about."

I still didn't feel any better. She hadn't said anything that would ease my pain. "You could've fucking called me when you saw that I wasn't there, Oshyn."

"It was so much going on, and everything happened so fast. I'm sorry, Chloe." She attempted to hug me, but I jerked away. "Look!" she said, waving her humongous rock in my face. "Isn't she pretty," Oshyn asked, turning it around to admire it again, probably for the millionth time. "How many carats do you think it is? I haven't had time to get it appraised.

She noticed the, 'I don't give a fuck' look on my face.

"Here, look," Oshyn said, as she handed me a stack of pictures. "I'm going to make a scrapbook out of them."

I snatched the pictures out of her hand, and got angrier as I saw pictures of people that we grew up with in Rochester. Pictures of fake paparazzi, the doves flying, the hot air balloon, and her new car wrapped in a big red bow. When I reached the picture of Grandma and that bitch Apples standing by her side as Brooklyn was on one knee, I got even angrier. I threw all the pictures in the air, and headed toward my car.

"Chloe, wait," she said, grabbing my arm. "I know you're upset, but honestly I didn't know you weren't going to be there."

"Get the fuck off me!" I yelled. "You're the only family I got, and you disrespected me by having that bitch stand beside you during the biggest moment in your life! Fuck you!" I was mad that she even decided to show me the pictures, like that was going to make me feel better.

I pulled my arm away, walked to my car, and sped off. I had enough of Apples. It seemed like she was always in the way, but I had something for her ass. As I drove away, I could see Oshyn in my rear view mirror picking the pictures up off the ground.

*I should make a u-turn and run her ass over*, I thought.

# 14

# CHLOE

Her grave looked rusty and old. *Mahogany Rodriguez,* the headstone read in fancy script writing. Her only family had moved away from Rochester and rarely came to visit. She had been abandoned once again. It had been eighteen years since her death, and I still missed her dearly. I did my best to straighten up her home before I sold it, but the damage was already done; bullet holes everywhere. I dropped down to my knees and let the tears fall for the only person who ever loved me.

I remembered the days when she used to gently comb my hair and sing me her favorite songs. I remembered how sweet she used to smell when she hugged me goodnight. I remembered…

"Chloe," a voice said from behind me. I looked up, wiping the tears from my eyes, trying to figure out who would dare interrupt my time with my mother.

"Quon? How'd you know I was here?"

"I do my research," he said straight faced.

He was the only reason I was in Rochester. I flew home because he had someone call to say that he needed to see me. I hadn't been back home since I moved to North Carolina. There was nothing here for me anymore.

He could have easily called me himself, but he didn't trust phones. He never even carried one on him, afraid that 'them boys' would use the GPS tracking device to hunt him down. Maybe that's why he's been free all this time, he always took extra precaution.

At thirty-four, he was strikingly handsome. He wore a new goatee to accompany his ceaser that showed off his premature gray hair. They say that gray hair at a young age is good luck, and I believed it, seeing as though he should've been dead a long time ago. He had made it to see thirty, which not too many people in our hood could say.

"Let's walk," he said, not waiting for me to get up. *I wonder why he chose the graveyard to be our meeting place*, I asked myself, but he was unpredictable. Maybe he figured that no one would check for him here.

I got up, said my goodbyes to Mom, and proceeded to catch up with him on the dusty gravel.

"How's my baby, Apples, doing?" Quon asked sincerely, waiting for an answer.

I never understood why niggas that beat their women would never leave them alone. He had become obsessed with her, his mind drowned with her image every second of the day. He could have any woman in the world, he was worth millions, but he was stuck on this bitch.

I lied. "She a'ight. Got a nigga though, and she even got the baby calling that man daddy. I heard he got a little paper and he gives her anything she wants. She looks happy."

His nostrils flared up, lips got tight, and breathing got a little heavier. He was losing control right in front of me, and I enjoyed every second of it.

"Word?" he said, shocking the hell out of me. That was a response I didn't expect to hear. It was like he had a split personality. "Well, I'm going to make this brief. I want Brooklyn dead."

"Brooklyn? How do you know him?" I asked, surprised that his name was known this far up north.

"I sent the nigga to handle Apples for me. Paid him well, two hundred and fifty thousand. He was supposed to bring her and the baby to me without arousing suspicion. I had a home-made dungeon built under my new house in Pittsford just for her. Got her wedding dress ready too." He didn't crack a smile. "She was finally going to be mine forever," he said, getting a little too excited. "But Brooklyn fucked the plan up."

This man had really lost his mind. He should have been off the streets and maybe even in a straight jacket. I remained quiet, because from the way he was acting, I didn't think that it was safe to talk. He was in a zone, a dangerous one.

"This faggot ass nigga ends up falling in love with your cousin, Oshyn, and proposing to her. What part of the game is that?"

"I feel you, yo. I was definitely in my feelings about that shit, too, but that's another story for another time."

"Anyways," he said, not caring about my personal problems. "I guess he called himself not following through, protecting the bitch because of Oshyn and shit." He looked me in the eyes and continued. "I want him to disappear. Bring Apples and Bella to me, alive. I'll give you one hundred grand. Fifty thousand now, and the rest when the job is done."

"Disappear?" I asked. "Like kill him?"

He looked around, making sure we weren't being watched. He never answered my question verbally, but his eyes said yes. I followed his stare; noticing a burial taking place. Whoever it was, finally at rest.

He took the Louis knapsack he had been carrying off and handed it to me.

"It's all there. Fifty thousand in cash."

"Why me?" I asked, wondering what he was up to.

Quon was a smart dude, feared by many and conquered by none. He could have easily killed Brooklyn by himself and ran off with Apples and the baby. I wanted to know why he wanted my help.

"Brooklyn is a beast. That's why I choose him for this job. He's experienced and one of the best in the game.

He is rarely distracted, and takes pleasure in his work. He expects me to retaliate because he knows how much this meant to me. It wasn't business — it was personal. He also knows that he's made an enemy for life. If I know him as well as I think I do, he has a hit out on me now, so he doesn't have to spend the rest of his natural life looking over his shoulder for me. He would never expect you to be his demise."

"Whoa...should I be offended by that comment?" I asked, offended regardless of his answer.

"Yeah...you're reckless and emotional. But money talks and at the right price I know you'll get the job done."

We walked back to our cars in silence. I could hardly think straight with all that money in my hands. The paper was coming in steady and without too much effort. With Brooklyn still holding on to the agreement we made, I didn't have to struggle anymore. All the money I had would be clean in no time. He pissed me off with the whole engagement deal, but I was beginning to think he was trying to protect me. Maybe that's why he didn't invite me. He had feelings for me all along and didn't want to hurt me.

I didn't feel bad for Apples either, she deserved what she had coming. I looked over my shoulder and blew my mother a kiss. I looked at the grave, wondering if she got it. I knew I wouldn't be able to see her for a while, but she lived in my heart.

CRACK!

Was all I heard before I hit the gravel covered in black snow. I looked up and saw Quon standing over me with a gun in his hand. *This crazy ass nigga just banged me in the head with the butt of his gun,* I said to myself, as I tried to stay alert. I never even saw him take it out. I held the gash on the top off my head with my hand while blood trickled down my face. I was having trouble trying to stay alert. Too scared to move, too painful to cry, I just sat there waiting for his next move.

He wrapped my hair around his hand and snatched me up off the ground, pressing the cold steel against my cheek and using it to pry my lips open.

"Umph," was all I could muster out, with the gun making itself at home in my mouth. My breathing sped up, showing itself in the cold air and panic struck my body. *I'm going to die here,* was all I could think about. Quon had no conscious, so pleading for my life, I knew, was out of the question.

"If you even think about fucking me over, bitch, I will kill you! I'll blow your fucking brains out. Brooklyn tried the shit, but he'll pay, and you will too..."

I was relieved, thinking that the abuse was over, when he took the gun out my mouth, but the fear came back when he picked me up and slammed me on the hood of his rusted blue Honda. He told me to take my pants off, and I didn't hesitate as I stared down the barrel of his gun. He spread my legs open and pressed the gun against my naked pussy. I hardly ever wore panties.

"Better yet, I'll blow your pussy out, that way you won't die right away. I like to torture," he said, as he fondled me with the tip of the gun. In a sick sort of way, he was turning me on. My head was spinning and the gash from the top of my head had resembled a bloody waterfall.

He forced the hard metal slightly in my pussy, tearing me a little. I rotated my hips slightly, giving him the okay to go further. I loved this freaky shit. I was scared to death, but needed to feel him inside of me. I laid on the hood of the freezing car and followed the motions of him sliding the gun in and out of my pussy. He pulled it out and shoved it back into my mouth. I wasn't sure whether to moan or scream.

He cocked it back and pulled the trigger.

# 15

# OSHYN

"I now pronounce you husband and wife," the pastor said aloud.

I smiled and kissed Brooklyn for what seemed like ten minutes. No one believed us when we told them to meet us at the Justice of the Peace, but a quick wedding was the perfect thing to do. If things had gone my way, I would have married Brooklyn's fine ass a few nights ago, at the engagement party because it was so romantic. I didn't understand why we couldn't.

Our pastor was there, and we had a million witnesses, but someone explained to me that we had to go through a licensing process to tie the knot.

Instead, I ended up taking this route. Brooklyn knew I wanted a lavish wedding, but said he wanted to be my husband now. My Grandmother, Apples, Micah and Bella stood by my side while I made one of the biggest commitments of my life.

I knew I'd have some explaining to do once people found out. Hell, I hated explaining myself to people. I'm a grown ass woman, I shouldn't have to justify myself to anyone, but I did feel bad about not telling Chloe. Even though it was a breath of fresh air that she wasn't there, I still felt bad that I hadn't invited her. She was, after all, my cousin. The only one I had.

I was still in disbelief that I had gotten married. I was a woman scorned, committed to never trust again, and then Brooklyn came from out of nowhere and stole my heart. *Finally*, I reasoned with myself, *it's my time to be happy.*

My Grandma was skeptical about the whole thing, but she tried her best to mind her business. I remember her asking me the day after the party, why we got engaged so fast. I took a deep breath, held her aging hand, and told her that we only lived once. I told her that he made me happy, and just when I thought I couldn't love again, I finally found my soul mate. He treats Micah like he's his son, and he makes a lot of money, which means he's not out to put a hole in my pockets.

That was reason enough, seeing as though I was always protecting myself from men who didn't make as much money as me.

I was also happy to tell Grandma that Brooklyn felt the same way about Chloe as she did, that's why he didn't invite her to the party. I thought I had solidified the deal by letting her know that she wasn't the only person who didn't trust Chloe, but she still wasn't moved. Actually, it looked like Grandma could have cared less. There was something that she wasn't telling me. Something was on the tip of her tongue that she wanted to tell me, but she hadn't seen me this happy in a while. I guess she'd rather keep it like that than to burden me with her constant warnings. I knew she meant well, but I was glad that she decided to keep her comments to herself, at least for that day.

❀　❀　❀

DING DONG!

"Coming!" I yelled to Apples, forgetting we had a brunch date today. *We needed to talk about my four minute wedding yesterday*, I thought, laughing to myself.

"Auntie !" Bella sang, with a toothless grin. I yanked on her curly golden ponytails until she snatched them away. They damn near touched her butt. Bella was so pretty and looked a lot like her father.

It's funny how we carry our kids for nine months, push their big heads out of our vaginas, and they still manage to be a mirror image of the men that cause us the most pain. I commend Apples though. She refused to treat Bella any different, even if she was the splitting image of the man who threatened to end her life.

"Where's Micah?" Bella asked, ready to find her

playmate.

"He's upstairs taking a nap. Go wake him up and tell him to get ready to go."

"Okay," Bella said, bouncing up the stairs.

"So, where are we going to eat?" Apples asked, rubbing her growling stomach.

"I'm in the mood for soul food, let's hit this spot downtown."

"Hell, yeah, their food is good as a bitch!"

I threw my hair back in a ponytail, put on some True Religion jeans, a white T, my North Face, and guarded my eyes from the sun with my studded out Chanel shades. Micah, trying to prove his independence, had dressed himself, and was waiting by the door.

We made our way out the house and drove to the restaurant. The host greeted us and showed us to our seats. We checked the menu out, trying to decide between the Soul food side, or Caribbean food.

"I think I'm going to have the turkey wings with collard greens and cornbread," I said.

"I'll probably get the Escovitch Red Snapper. I saw somebody eating that shit last week and it looked banging."

"Last week? You come here too much."

"You know I can't cook, bitch," she said unashamed.

Apples wasn't lying either. Her ass couldn't boil water. The nigga, Quon, had her sitting so pretty that he forbid her to touch any of that. He provided her with four meals a day, and a round the clock housekeeper. She was spoiled rotten, but it came at a price that, in the end, wasn't worth paying.

"Guess what?" she asked.

"Yeah?"

"I got accepted into UNC Law program!" She handed me her acceptance papers, as if I wouldn't have believed her.

"Oh, my goodness, babe! Congratulations! When did this happen?" I asked, reaching over the kids to give her a hug. I was so happy for her.

"It's something that I always wanted to do, and I think I'm stable enough to go ahead. I have your grandma to help with Bella, and I've saved a nice amount of money from the generous salary that you pay me, so I won't have to take out a loan."

"So, what kind of lawyer do you want to be?" I asked, with a mouth full of bread.

"Well, first I was thinking about entertainment law. There's a lot of money out there and I always wanted to be in the industry. Then I thought about being a real estate lawyer, so that we could keep everything in house."

"That would be great!" I said, thinking of all the good that would do the company. "Keep it in the family," I added, counting all the bread that we would make together.

"I know. Those are the things that I would love to do,

but what's really set in my heart is to represent domestic abuse victims. Oshyn, you know I always had a lot of money, but when Quon started fucking me up, I couldn't run because I couldn't afford it. It paralyzed me. He's not rich, the nigga is wealthy, and he kept me poor and dependent on him. I want to help other girls who are in the same situation that I'm in. Girls that can't afford to get the help, but genuinely want to get out. If it weren't for you, I would've ended up burnt alive like that chick whose husband poured a Sprite bottle full of gasoline all over her."

Her eyes watered up again. This was a subject that the devil had waged a war against in her mind.

"Babe, maybe you should go to counseling," I suggested, watching her struggle with the hurt that she refused to let go of. I handed her a tissue so the kids wouldn't notice her crying.

"Nah, I'm good," she said, with a slight sniffle. "I'm moving on, really."

"Alright, if you say so."

We devoured our food, leaving nothing but bones on the plate. I grabbed the bill, paid it, and we left. We drove to Triangle Town Center Mall, did a little shopping and sat down while the kids played in the fun house.

"I think I'm gonna build a house, somewhere in Chapel Hill near the school."

"That's way too far. Then you'll have to drive all the

way back here just to drop Bella off before you go to work. Why don't you just build your crib in Raleigh and drive to Chapel Hill? It's only a thirty minute drive, I think."

Maybe she was just thinking pre-maturely, but her mind was definitely moving a mile a minute, trying to get her plans for the future together. We talked for a bit more and decided to head on back home.

We were seconds away from our car when we heard a bitch say, "Yo, ain't that Brooklyn's new wife?"

"Yeah, that's her. Fuck that bitch!"

I frowned and turned around to see who was getting ready to get it. I wasn't too surprised when I saw his miserable ass ex, Shante, and five of her homegirls. It was becoming kind of corny that they still traveled in packs like that.

"The nigga probably out fucking her cousin, Chloe, as we speak," one girl said. "I heard that he had her on his team," another one added.

My first instinct was to swing, but quickly realized that the kids were still with me. I glanced over at Apples, and like a pit bull, she was ready for the kill. I waved to Shante slowly, with Apples right beside me, and forced a slight smile on my face.

With my thumbs in my front pocket, and a stance that I used as leverage when I go to rock a bitch, I said to Shante, "Don't be mad that you been sucking the nigga dick all this time and he married me without hesitation, you bum bitch!"

They surrounded us. Guess she thought that with all the bitches she had with her, I was going to back down, but she had the wrong bitch. I glanced over at the kids, who were still by my side, and pushed them out the way toward a parked car.

I sized up all the bitches, figuring that I could take most of them. The good thing about being jumped was that everybody was swinging at each other and never the intended target.

Shante stared at me with a look of betrayal. To her, I was the reason that she and Brooklyn weren't together. That's so funny about us women. It was never the man's fault, always ours. The woman you never knew, the complete stranger, the one that doesn't owe you anything. She had the same look on her face that I had plenty of times when confronted with Trent's bitches. The look of revenge, hate and murder.

"Bum bitch? Oh, I got your bum bitch..."

I cocked my hand back, ready for the kill when all the bitches backed up. It was too many of them to be scared of me, so I knew something was up. I turned sideways to check out the activity behind me, when I saw Apples toting the glock by her side.

"It's broad daylight, Apples," I said, reminding her that we were still outside the mall. I wanted to rock the broads, but Apples' deranged look had me scared.

"I don't give a fuck. Jump bitches!" she said, moving

past me toward the gang of punks.

"That bitch ain't gonna do shit," one girl said, assuring herself that Apples wasn't that stupid.

Apples cocked the .357 back and aimed it at her head. The bystanders screamed, and scrambled in all directions.

"Apples, fuck them hoes. Give me the gun and let's get out of here." I was a little nervous myself. I didn't even know she had started carrying a gun again. She was one person they shouldn't have given a license to, but with her perfect record, they couldn't say no.

Her face was tight and her body was stiff. Apples stared off in a daze, and my hand movements couldn't bring her out of it. I knew I needed to rush though, because I was sure the police had been called.

"Mommy!" Bella said, running towards her mother at full speed.

Apples came out of her trance and lowered the gun. She gave her daughter a hug, and without speaking, walked off with Bella in one hand and the gun in the other. Shante and her homegirls just stared in disbelief as she quietly walked by, none of them daring to utter a word to her. I quickly swooped Micah up, rushed to the car, and we all sped away, leaving skid marks on the pavement.

"When did you start carrying a gun?" I asked, on our way back home.

"For protection," she answered, and it was silence

from then on.

Silence.

Dead Silence.

❈  ❈  ❈

"You need to put your bitches in check!" I screamed at Brooklyn, as soon as he walked through the door. I had called him to come over as soon as Apples left the house. He hadn't officially moved in with us yet, and may be banned before we combined our households.

"What are you talking about?" he asked confused. He reached to hug me, but I pushed him away. "Baby what's up?"

"I'm out with my kids, and your bitch, Shante, steps to me with five other bitches! I'm out with my kids, and the bitch is trying to jump me? What kind of shit is that? And then the bitch says something about you fucking Chloe!" I knew that wasn't true, but I just wanted to throw that out there to let him know how disrespectful the lying bitch was being.

He hadn't said a thing. Just sat on the micro fiber ottoman and rubbed on his chin.

"Then my best friend risks her life and her freedom by aiming a gun at the bitch's head at two o'clock in the afternoon at the mall!" By now I was steaming. I paced the floor, ready to clock Brooklyn's ass. "Had Shante or anyone else said one more thing, they would've been dead. I couldn't even calm Apples down. It took Bella calling her name to make her realize what she was doing."

He was still rubbing his chin and staring at the carpet, apparently in deep thought.

"You're not going to have me in no fucked up situations where I have to watch my back with my son!"

"He's my son too," he said, as he stood up. He grabbed me by the waist, looked me in the eyes and said, "First off, the bitch, Shante, just wants to have something to say. But I can assure you that you'll never have this problem again. Is Apples okay?" he asked, nibbling on my neck.

"I don't know. When she left, she wouldn't say much. I didn't even know she had a gun. I guess she started carrying it, just in case Quon showed up. I think the reality of her actually having to use it hit her hard, and she couldn't handle it."

Brooklyn made his way up to my ear, and the hairs on my neck started to stand. He was done talking about Shante, and apparently on to me.

"Look, baby, I've got to run and take care of some business, but I'm sorry about today. You'll never have to go through that again. And that's word to my mother. I'm going to take care of that bitch."

I kissed his lips, happy that he had promised to rectify the situation. "What kinda business you gotta take care of?" I asked, feeling his crotch.

"Come on, baby," he said, inching toward the door, "I gotta pick up some money for this event I've invested in. As a matter of fact, it's a party in Miami. The shit is next week, so have your bags packed." He tried his best to escape, but I grabbed his collar tightly. "Ask Apples if she wants to go too," he said.

"I tell you what, do something with this, and I'll ask her," I said, pointing to my body.

He owed me for allowing that bitch to stress me out, and I wasn't going to let him go that easily. He walked over toward me, lifting his shirt over his head in the process. His perfectly cut chocolate body told the tale of a man who sacrificed hours out of his day to maintain his physique. When he got close enough, I held him by the crease in his back as he kissed every inch of my neck with his soft damp lips.

"I've wanted you all day," he said, as he stopped to undress me.

"Prove it," I replied back, giving him the okay to do whatever he pleased.

Instantly, he picked me up, carried me to our bedroom, and gently placed me on the bed. Pressing his warm naked body against mine, he played with my lips, allowing his tongue to dance in my mouth. His big dick grew long and hard, while it rested on my leg. We both wanted it in, but we loved the foreplay. I rolled my head back while he nibbled on the base of my neck.

"Ahhhh," I gasped, as my body tingled all over.

I loved how the slight roughness of his fingers felt against the silkiness of my breasts. I moaned as he wrapped his lips around my nipples. He handled me with such care and love, proving he didn't have the need to get too aggressive. He took his time, marking his territory with his tongue while drenching my entire body.

"Give it to me!" I said, as I bit my lower lip. I wasn't able to tolerate the wait any longer and needed to feel him inside of me. "Put it inside my pussy," I whined, as he ignored my words.

"You like that?" he asked, as he stuck the head of his dick inside of me.

"I love it!" I dug my nails in his back, as he thrust his dick all the way inside of my wet hole. "Give me more!"

He moved his body to the rhythm of mine, making sure that I enjoyed every inch of pleasure he was determined to give. To me, this was worth the wait. I was finally with a man that loved and cherished me, and meant more than just a fuck to him. Every time he touched me, we made love.

"Shit," he said, as I squeezed my muscles tightly on his dick. My sudden action caused him to stroke harder. Suddenly, he flipped around on his back, and directed me to ride him. I slowly moved back and forth, taking his hand and resting it on my pussy.

"Touch me," I said, as he began to massage my clit. My pace got faster, and I pinched my nipples, trying to get as much pleasure as I could. "I can't take no more!" I screamed, no longer in control of the situation. He never let up on rubbing my clit and I was ready to explode. "Daddy, come with me!"

He pumped faster, as my riding got more aggressive and off beat. I had never had a man give it to me like this before.

"Aaahhhhhh!" I screamed, as my body tensed up.

I collapsed on top of his and froze for a moment trying to recoup from all the energy that I'd just lost. Our breathing was still heavy as we attempted to get our composure together. I looked up at him as he dozed off into la la land. I gently kissed his face, being careful not to wake him and closed my eyes too. *I guess he's going to miss his meeting*, I snickered.

# 16

# CHLOE

I had been back in North Carolina for a week, and no one knew of my whereabouts except for Joy. Together, we plotted on kidnapping Apples and Bella, and struggled with a *how to plan* on getting rid of Brooklyn. With my forehead the size of a golf ball, there was no way I could hide what happened to me. Everyone would have too many questions that I couldn't answer, so I stayed at the Hilton Hotel, hoping the swelling would go down, and trying to come up with a plan to handle Brooklyn and Apples.

Quon had me nervous as hell. Every few seconds, I would run toward the peephole, checking to see if anyone stood outside my room. To my surprise, nothing.

Lately, it really hit me that I've been living a double life. With all the money that I had accumulated from different men, I could buy anything. But material things hadn't come without risk.

Mr. Bourdeaux, I'm sure was looking for me. He is worth billions, and the picture that I have of him would, without a doubt, ruin his life. The money he paid me was nothing to him, chump change, and yet, I knew that he wasn't satisfied.

He was very familiar with the game of blackmail. Just because I gave him a copy of the picture didn't mean it was the *ONLY* copy. I've probably got a hit out on me now, and needed to watch every move.

And Quon was the devil himself. I knew that after this job was done, I would have to leave the state, maybe even the country. I would have to start a new life and maybe even start a family. *Humph. That didn't sound too bad,* I thought to myself. *A family.* I was straight forever. I just had to play my cards right so that I could get out of this mess alive.

I laid back, closed my eyes, and thought about Brooklyn. I wondered if I was doing the right thing. Part of me, the part that loved him, wanted to tell him everything I knew. I wanted to tell him about Quon and the hit on his life. I wanted to tell him I had been paid to take him out. I wondered if he'd accept an offer to run away with me instead.

But the other part of me, the one that knows he doesn't give a fuck about me, said to shut the fuck up. That side told me to do what I agreed to do and keep it moving. Part of me wanted to risk defying Quon for true love, and the other part said fuck true love.

The moment my cell phone rung, I answered on the first ring. Even though it said unknown, I couldn't take any chances on missing the call. I had to do everything on schedule. One wrong move would mess me up for life. Literally!

"Yo?" I said, in a groggy voice, pretending like I was asleep.

"WHERE THE FUCK YOU AT?" Beef screamed through the receiver. I was instantly pissed that I allowed him to trick me.

"Hey, baby," I said, as sweet as I could. I knew that I was on my last string with Beef and needed to be on my best behavior. I couldn't afford for my shady life to be uncovered.

"Don't fucking baby me! Where the fuck you been at, bitch?"

"Bitch?" I said crying. I knew this had to be one of the best performances that the world had ever seen. "It was my mother's birthday and I went to visit her grave," I cried even harder. Still sniffling, I continued. "This is something that I'm not over yet, and I just wanted to be by myself." I lied.

"Why didn't you ask me to go with you, Chloe?" he asked, softening up his tone.

"I needed to be alone. You know, get myself together. I'm too old for the bullshit I'm doing. Same shit, different day." Even though I was running game on Beef, the shit I was talking sounded good. *So true.*

"You could've told me you weren't going to be coming home for a while."

"Baby, I'm sorry, but I've been dealing with a few things lately. Please forgive me? I...I love you!" I knew if nothing else would get him, the 'L' word would.

Beef was from the 'dirt', which is the hood in the country. He was a street nigga, but he was one that wanted to be in love. He thought he could turn a hoe into a housewife. He refused to believe that people like me couldn't be changed. It was in our blood. He didn't want a good girl either, he wanted a woman he could tame. One he had to chase.

"Whatever, Chloe! I'm getting real sick of your shit!" he said, right before he hung up.

I was satisfied with the way the conversation ended. The mere fact that he didn't say not to come back home was validation that I was still in good. He was mad, but I had ways to make him get over it.

I sat up in my bed, and reached for my purse. I checked for my crumbled up letter from Aunt Rosalyn and my newly acquired 9 millimeter. I cocked it back just to make sure it was working fine when my phone screamed again. It startled me. Then again, everything was starting to startle me. *When did I turn this shit up so loud?* I wondered, knowing it was Beef calling me again. Whenever he hung up so suddenly, he always called back to either apologize or add another comment to prove his point.

"Open the door! I'm in the hall."

I panicked and my panties moistened at the same time.

Every since Quon's gun dug up in my pussy, fear was the only thing that could get me wet. It was satisfying, in a sick sort of way. The thought of the blow to the head brought me back to reality. So, I crept to the door. The reaction of the person on the other side would either be able to make my job easy or do me no good.

I snatched the door open with my gun cocked to the side. Before he could say a word, I rammed my tongue down his throat and kissed him as hard as I could. He looked so different since the last time I'd seen him. He pushed me away, making me fall on the bed. I needed him in the worst way.

Although we needed to discuss business, his smell had me hypnotized. I needed him to hear my plan. I needed him to say everything would be okay. But all I heard were the sounds of him devouring me. For some reason today, for the first time, I wanted to be held. I no longer wanted to be the mistress to anyone. All the money in the world, wouldn't satisfy my instant need for love.

But at the end of the day, I knew I'd still be lonely and yearning for a genuine touch. *My cousin was happy*, I sulked. She made a decent amount of change, the honest way, and she did a fine job of raising her son. She even had a husband...a husband that made her smile.

Those are the things that I wanted for my life.

Instead, I got fucked on the floor like a horny dog in heat. For hours, we switched positions like we were lovers instead of there to make a deal. When it was all said and done, I punked out.

"I can't do it," I revealed.

❀    ❀    ❀

I went home to Beef about four days later, which made my absence from him about a week and a half. I knew I would have a lot of kissing up to do, but I needed to make sure that my injury had healed.

I stopped by the grocery store and gathered the things that I needed to make a romantic candle lit dinner. I also dropped an EPT test into the cart. My period, which was nowhere to be found, was scheduled to come sometime last week and I had been feeling nauseous lately. I knew something wasn't right, but I wanted to be sure before I started making any decisions. I went home, bathed, and put on my white silk knee length robe with nothing underneath.

I slaved over the stove, preparing two huge lobster tails and a roast, which were both his favorite meals. While the roast cooked and the lobster tails marinated, I went to the bathroom, peed in the cup, and stuck the white stick inside. Too anxious to just sit there and wait, I went back to the kitchen and checked on the food. As my phone rang, I jetted over to check the name first. I had to make sure it wasn't Quon trying to be slick, and didn't want to miss Beef's call.

He didn't know that I had come home, and I didn't want to piss him off anymore by not answering his calls. I looked on the caller ID and saw that the caller was Oshyn. I contemplated on whether or not to answer the phone. I was anxious to talk to her, but nonetheless, still angry.

I figured I would answer, so I wouldn't have to be the one to call her back, which to me, was a sign of weakness.

"Yeah," I answered, as cold and as dry as my voice would allow.

"Hey, Chloe, it's me, Oshyn," she said, as if I wouldn't recognize her voice.

"Yeah," I repeated.

"Look, I'm sorry about the whole wedding thing. I honestly didn't know anything about it, but you were right. Once I was there and realized that you weren't, I should've called and told you to come. You're my family, and I don't want any bad blood between us, so can we *pleaseeeeeeee* forget this whole mess?"

I was tempted to accept her apology and move on, but I didn't want to seem too desperate and so eager to forgive. She was, after all my cousin, and it wasn't her fault, but I didn't want to seem like a chump.

"It's easy for you to forget, Oshyn, but the whole

thing is fucked up! You put everything before blood, even that bitch Apples."

"Watch your mouth," she said, ready to defend her friend's honor. "Look, I ain't call here to fight with you, I tried calling to make amends. I'm going to Miami this weekend with Brooklyn. I was going to ask Apples if she wanted to go, but she has plans, so do you want to go? You can consider it an all expense paid apology, and you can tell Beef to come too."

"Oh, so now I'm your sloppy seconds? The bitch don't want to go, so you come to me as your last resort? Fuck you!" I hung up, hoping she liked hearing dial tones.

In my mind she was trying to play me, but I had enough. I was ready to move forward with the plans to erase Apples out of our lives forever. I finished up with the dinner and set the table as fast as I could. Beef would be here any minute, and I wanted everything to be perfect.

*Oh shit, the test,* I said to myself, as I ran to the bathroom. *That was real sloppy, thank God I remembered,* I thought as I wondered how much damage my forgetfulness would do. I grabbed the white stick that determined my fate and saw what I had concluded all along. Positive.

I had a phone call to make. Looks like I was going to Miami after all.

# 17

# OSHYN

It was nice to get away. Away from the office, away from the drama, just away from everything. My real estate business was booming, and although the money was great, this was a well-needed vacation, even if it was for only three days.

I had fifteen minutes to meet Chloe in the lobby of our hotel, the La Jasondra. Whoever named the spot was obviously drunk, but whoever designed the hotel, had done so with elegance and grace. Fourteen carat gold faucets laced every room, along with the world's most expensive granite, hardwood and wrought iron.

Brooklyn had arranged for us to stay in one of the Presidential suites, which was absolutely breathtaking. It's amazing how much that man spoiled me. Chloe and I had made plans to go on a shopping spree, so that we could have some 'girl time' before the guys woke up.

I'm not sure what the sudden change of heart was,

but I was glad she decided to come. This was some well deserved bonding time that the both of us could use. I was looking at some people relaxing by the pool when the phone rang. I decided to take the call from the phone in the bathroom.

"What's up girl?" I asked, knowing it was Chloe.

"What in the hell are you doing?" she asked aggravated.

"I just finished sucking Brooklyn's dick!" I said frustrated.

"Well, I know he's pissed. I heard you needed some work on your head game." Chloe said, laughing in my ear.

"Shut up!" I was only joking.

"Don't you know it's not nice to joke with grown people? Get dressed."

I sucked my teeth and hung up the phone. I hated to be rushed. I took a quick shower and threw on my classic white linen Christian Dior sundress and Jimmy Choo flat lace up sandals. The forecast read ninety-eight degrees, so I put some sunscreen on my cherry brown skin, and threw my long hair into a ponytail. I went over to the bed and kissed Brooklyn gently on the forehead. *My baby looks so good when he sleeps.* I picked up the money laying on the nightstand and noticed it was only two thousand dollars. That obviously wasn't going to be enough, so I went to Brooklyn's stash in the safe and took out ten g's. *I don't know why he travels with all this money, but it works in my favor today,* I thought to myself, as I headed out the door.

When the elevator doors opened, the first person I saw was Chloe. She wore her usual hoochie-mama booty shorts, with a sheer hot pink shirt that exposed her lace bra.

"I hate going places with you. You're so slow," Chloe said, upset that she had to wait for thirty minutes.

"Listen, you're not going to fuck up my vacation with all the damn complaining, so be easy."

"Whatever!" she said, rolling her eyes.

"Oh, by the way, nice purse," I said, holding up my bag to show Chloe that we were carrying the same Hermes bag.

"You just love to bite my style," she responded, walking out the lobby.

We walked outside and were greeted by the pounding heat and humid air of South Beach. I paused and gazed at the palm trees. *When I get home, I want to plant some of those in my backyard. That's the real reason I moved down south anyway. I thought North Carolina had palm trees.*

"You want to walk down Collins Avenue?" I asked.

"Hell no! Do you feel this heat?" she answered, amazed that I had even entertained the idea. We waited for our valet to retrieve the rental, a white 2007 Cadillac Escalade.

"Excuse me, sir," I asked the young chubby valet.

"Where's the hottest place to shop?"

"Bal Harbor Mall," he answered, in his thick Bahamian accent.

"Thanks," I said.

When the car arrived, Oshyn and I spent another ten minutes arguing about who was going to drive. At that moment I was beginning to regret asking her to come with me on this trip. Oshyn was always trying to be on rock star status. I hope she wasn't telling herself that I was a damn chauffer. Reluctantly, I decided to hop in the driver's seat to avoid any further drama. We drove down Ocean Drive, taking in the scenery until we reached our destination.

"I can't believe I've spent eight thousand already," I said, looking into my purse to check my funds. That was a bad habit of mine. I loved to shop, and the majority of my money went on shoes and purses...expensive ones.

"Girl, that's chump change. I can spend that in ten minutes," Chloe said, laughing.

"You hungry?" I asked, rubbing my growling stomach, ignoring her hating ass comment.

"As hell!"

We walked over to a restaurant called the *Panini Café* to grab a bite to eat.

"Damn, twenty-four dollars for a salad? That's crazy!" I said. No matter how much money I spent, I was still from the hood and couldn't imagine paying that much for a salad.

"Bitch, don't act like that. We're Queens, and Queens eat twenty-four dollar salads, buy six thousand dollar purses, drive hundred thousand dollar cars and..."

"Alright. Shut up," I mumbled to Chloe, obviously aggravated. "What do you have planned for the rest of the day?" I asked, hoping she would exclude herself from Brooklyn and I.

"Well, Beef will probably want to eat, fuck, and go back to sleep, so I'll probably sneak out, take a few ecstasy pills, and hit up the strip clubs. You should come with me," she said, anxious for an answer.

"Nah," I replied nonchalantly. "I'm good." I always declined. It just wasn't something that I was into. It was amazing how different we were.

"What, you think you too good?" she stated, upset by another let down. "I don't know why, because you should know that Brooklyn is fucking other bitches! Don't get brand new and forget how niggas with money get down. Just because you're his wife, and he gave you access to his stash, don't mean that you're the only one. You're number one, but never the only one. Let me find out that you're dick whipped and forgot all the rules. Let's not forget about Trent and how that turned out."

I looked at Chloe, as she smiled from ear to ear. *How could she bring up a situation that I'm trying to erase? And why is this bitch smiling about it? Chloe was always trying to throw salt in my game*, I thought.

"Whatever, bitch! I'm happy, and I can get money

with or without Brooklyn, so fuck you," I said, giving her the middle finger. I hated talking to her about my relationship. It was something that always made me uncomfortable, something about the situation sent chills up my spine.

In between our arguments, Brooklyn called to let me know that he and Beef were leaving to take care of some business.

*So much for Chloe sneaking out.*

"Do you have enough money, baby? I see you took a nice piece of change?" he asked.

"No daddy, I'm running low," I said, in my baby voice.

"Well, I'll leave more in the safe in you need it," he said.

"Alright, I love you."

"Love you too."

"I think I'm going to throw up!" Chloe said, with her hand over her mouth after I hung up.

I motioned for the waiter to come to our table.

"Sir, can I order a large glass of haterade for the young lady?" I said smiling.

Chloe and I couldn't help but laugh as the waiter walked off, with a confused look on his face.

I glanced at my watch and noticed that it was almost six. Tired from the heat, shopping and food, Chloe and I decided to head back to our hotel to take a nap.

❋  ❋  ❋

I woke up three hours later, needing to call my grandma to make sure Micah was doing well. The clock in the room read eight o'clock, even though I knew it was nine. It was getting late. My grandmother was always in the bed by nine-thirty. The guys still hadn't gotten back yet, but I decided to wait before I called to check up on them. I went in my purse to get my cell phone, and noticed a small silver vibrator inside. *What the...*I thought as I took the vibrator out and examined it.

"This has to belong to Chloe. Who would be freaky enough to have a travel size vibrator?" I asked to myself, as I continued to look in the purse. After finally seeing her driver's license I realized that I had taken her purse by mistake.

I put her friend back in its home, and searched for Chloe's room key. I needed to get my purse back so I could call grandma. I refused to use the hotel phone. *How in the hell did she get in her room? She probably fucked some bellboy,* I thought.

I put on a wife beater, my La Perla boy shorts, and walked down the hall to her suite. Not bothering to knock, I slid the card in the slot and waited for the green light to come on. Letting myself in, I opened the door softly, so that it wouldn't slam, scaring her half to death.

When I entered the room, all the lights had been

turned off. As I searched for the switch, I could hear the sounds of Chloe moaning from the bedroom. *That's strange*, I thought. *I didn't know Beef was back already. Or is she fucking the bellboy*, I thought, laughing to myself.

"Uuuuuuggggggggghhhhhhh…it feels so good," I heard her moan again.

"Shit, she would be having sex when I need something," I said softly. "Let me get out of here."

I crept back toward the door. Seconds from leaving, I heard a familiar voice…

I tiptoed back in quietly, shutting the door. The room was lit with mango-scented candles, and the flames reflected off the walls. I peeked around the corner, trying to convince my heart not to believe my eyes.

She was on top.

He was laid back on the bed with his hands behind his head, enjoying the view. My vision became blurry and I almost blacked-out. I couldn't move, forcing myself to watch my husband, and my only cousin, both moan in pure ecstasy. She bent down and kissed him in the mouth with so much passion, like they had done this before. They had definitely done this before.

I turned on the lights and just stood there. The whole world froze for what seemed like an eternity, and everything seemed to happen in slow motion.

Brooklyn's gray eyes pierced my soul like they had the day we first met. He lowered his head and said absolutely nothing.

Chloe got off him with a look of satisfaction on her face. She never said it, but I knew. I was speechless, and murder was in my heart. I wanted someone to die. That was the only way that they would feel the way I did at this very moment.

"How could you?" I whispered, looking at the both of them.

Not expecting my next move, Brooklyn attempted to grab my fists that had already landed on his face. I'd fought men before and had beaten some of the best.

"I'm sorry, Oshyn," was the only thing he could muster up. I punched him again, this time in the mouth.

"That's my cousin!" I screamed, as if he didn't know.

"Baby, I'm sorry."

"Fuck you," I said, swinging again, this time landing my fist on his eye.

He tackled me, using the glass table next to the bed as a cushion. It shattered all over the place. My body was weak and my heart hurt. All I wanted was a hug, and the tackle sort of felt like one.

"Get the fuck off me," I said, trying to catch whatever air I could with his two hundred and fifty pound frame on top of me. "I can't breathe!"

"Oshyn, please just calm down," he said, lifting his sweaty naked body off me.

Then I looked up and saw her. Our eyes met. I wanted to kill her...she ruined my life.

"After all I've done for you?" Like I said before, funny

how we always wanted to blame the woman, but Chloe was my flesh and blood, and this was the ultimate betrayal.

There had always been rumors of Brooklyn fucking around. Your heart always knows...my heart never wanted to know. I remembered Shante's comment about Brooklyn fucking with Chloe. I can't believe I was that stupid! I guess I just wanted to choose my battles carefully before I ruined my new happy home.

I sunk my teeth into his damp, salty skin, and he quickly got off me. I jumped to my feet as fast as I could and ran toward Chloe. Grabbing a big chunk of her hair, I banged her head against the wall. Growing up with her, I had seen her beat bitches unconscious. When they saw her coming, they knew they were no match scraping with their hands, so they handled it with bats and knives.

Chloe put up a fight. She had always been slightly bigger than me, but she wasn't fighting the angry side of me. She was fighting my heart, and I was beating her ass. If it weren't for Brooklyn pulling me off of her, I would've killed her with my bare hands. It's crazy what everyone says they'll do in a situation like this. I was totally out of character, a stranger to myself, but then again, who wouldn't be? I completely understood the concept of temporary insanity. Today, I was temporarily insane.

"Oshyn, stop!" Brooklyn yelled. "Just go back to the room!"

*How dare he have the audacity to be mad and give me orders?* "Oshyn, just go back to the room," he repeated. "It's not what you think."

"I'm not going anywhere, you bitch ass nigga! Go suck a dick!" I said, tossing the black hotel phone at his head. He ducked, as if dodging a bullet.

Chloe grabbed her keys and headed to grab her purse. I snatched it away as I noticed her face. Evidence of our fight showed, with her busted lip and swollen eye. She and Brooklyn both had one.

"Where the fuck do you think you're going?" I snapped.

Looking like a mad woman and breathing like a Lucifer himself, I paced the suite, looking for something sharp. I ignored Brooklyn's constant apologies as he put on his pants.

"Don't question me, bitch! Handle this shit with your man," she said hatefully. "He got a lot to tell you. This isn't the first time!"

My mind went blank.

I picked up the cold nine-millimeter gun peeking from Chloe's purse. I held it as tightly as I could, with my palms sweating profusely.

*Why would she have a gun?* "No bitch, *YOU* got a lot to tell me!" I said, with the gun now aimed at her head.

Chloe dropped her hotel key and laughed as though she didn't care that she hurt me.

"Bitch, you don't scare me!" she shouted.

"You should be. You know how this shit goes! Déjà vu, don't you remember, or has it been that long ago?" I asked, reminding her of our deep dark family secret. The reason she s motherless and mine was in prison for the rest of her life. The ultimate betrayal — family.

"Oh yeah, I remember!" she said, tapping her bruised face with her index finger. "I remember Brooklyn sticking his big black dick in my big yellow pussy tonight…last week…last month too." She paused, while a big smile appeared on her face. She looked down and rubbed her stomach.

"And I'm surprised he hasn't told you that I'm pregnant with his baby!"

I pulled the trigger…I had heard enough. Again the world froze. Brooklyn tried to blend in with the wall, hoping not to be noticed. Chloe grabbed her stomach, trying to keep the blood in that was pouring out onto the floor.

*Good*, I reasoned. *She finally feels the pain that I felt.*

I spit on her squirming body and walked out of the room.

My vacation was over.

# 18

# OSHYN

After I shot her, I ran back to my room and packed my stuff. Although I hurried, I knew there was no rush because Brooklyn and Chloe would both die first before they called the police. However, I knew someone had to have heard the shots. I was out the hotel in ten minutes flat, grabbing only my identification, pocketbook, and Brooklyn's money left in the safe. I took it all, thirty-six thousand. I didn't want that motherfucker to be able to buy shit, not even a cab ride.

I exited the hotel from the side door, hoping nobody saw me. Once on the street, I hailed a taxi to the airport and stayed there until the ticket counter opened the next morning. While waiting, I called Beef to tell him what happened. He had family in Miami and was at the strip club when all of this was going down. He and Brooklyn weren't all that close, but on the strength they were both with cousins, they associated with each other.

"I walked in and saw them fucking, she was on top," I whispered through the phone, hoping if I said it low enough, the pain would go away. It wouldn't. I didn't tell him that I shot his girl, but I wanted him to know she fucked my man.

"I'm on my way there, yo. I'ma kill that bitch!" he shouted, probably more mad at all the bread he had spent on her than anything else.

"No, don't go. The police are probably all over there by now. Some shit went down and I'm leaving," I said, hoping he could sense my discreetness.

I wanted desperately to tell him about the shooting, but quickly wised up. As far as I was concerned, no one knew what happened except for Chloe and Brooklyn, and it was better that it stayed that way.

"Yeah, alright, that bitch will get hers," he said disappointed. He had no idea I'd already handled it. I felt like going back shooting the spot up with an uzie, even though I loved them both. I couldn't believe that this had happened.

❁   ❁   ❁

Days later, I was severely depressed, and all the drama that had been going on begun to take its toll on my body. Once thick in all the right places, I had lost ten pounds because I had no appetite. My grandmother insisted that I stay with her until I was well enough to be on my own, but I couldn't. I knew it would be the first place everyone would go to look for me, so I choose to stay at a hotel until things died down. The saying goes, *there's no bed like your own,* and it's completely right.

I thought about how much I missed my home, while I hugged the unfamiliar pillow in the strange bed that had become my best friend. I buried my face in it, and cried hard, trying to drown and suffocate myself out of my misery. Part of me didn't want to live anymore, so I contemplated ending the grief, figuring only then would I never hurt like this again. But the other part wouldn't let me.

I lifted my head off the wet pillow and tried to stand up. My weak and dehydrated body didn't have enough strength to hold me up. Suddenly, I collapsed back on the bed. I gave up, realizing that I wasn't ready to face the world yet, and decided to go to sleep, which I had been doing a lot of lately. I laid there, trying as hard as I could to doze off. My mind just wouldn't let go of all the images that haunted me from seeing Chloe and Brooklyn together.

Just as I was about to have another melt down, my grandmother called. No matter how much things got on my nerves, she was always there when I needed her the most.

"Hello?" I whispered. The stress had even lowered my voice box.

"Oshyn, come over and get some food," she said, in

a tone that let me know, *no* wasn't an option.

"But mama, I'm not hungry, I keep telling you that. I'm just tired," I pouted. "I just want to go to sleep." I was very irritated and she could tell.

"Ju watch jur tone with me! I will see ju here shortly," she said, reminding me who was in charge.

I'm pretty sure that she was sick of my recent back talk, but it wasn't personal. I really just didn't want to be bothered. Realizing that I had no other choice, I gathered what little strength I had, sluggishly got dressed and headed to her house.

❊ ❊ ❊

Lately, I had been unable to tolerate the smell of chicken. My grandmother was cooking some and it was making me sick to my stomach. I didn't use to be sensitive to everything, but recently my body was changing. *Maybe it's just from the added stress in my life*, I thought, as I fought the nausea that was trying to rear its ugly head.

Micah was out with Apples, and my grandmother did all she could to nurse me back to health. I told both of them what had happened a few weeks earlier. Apples was livid that she wasn't there, and I assured her that it was for the best that she wasn't. My grandmother was mad that I had even invited Chloe to Miami, insisting that she knew something like this was going to happen.

'Generational curse' is what she called it. Maybe it was.

I didn't care about any of it, I just wanted the nightmare to be over. I hadn't heard from Chloe, nor did I care to. I wasn't sure if she was dead, or in the hospital in Florida. I just wanted her to disappear from my life forever. She had caused too much pain in my life, just like her mom had done mine.

I thought back to that fateful night which determined the rest of our lives, and began to sob. My mother was such a good mom, and I only hoped to be half the mother to Micah that she was to me. She was so loving, so generous and so gentle. Even at seven years old, I remember her talking about her goals and how successful we were going to be. I use to share her joy of the future. Today, I share her pain of hopelessness.

I was upset at myself for jeopardizing the welfare of my family because of Chloe's betrayal, but the blame couldn't be placed all on me. I was still surprised of the person I had become when I saw the two of them together. I was simply not myself. A monster maybe, but not myself.

"Ju okay?" my grandmother asked, running her frail fingers through my frazzled hair.

"I don't know, mama, everything is wrong. How could she...how could he?" I asked, as I broke down. "They say what goes around comes around, but what have I done in my life to warrant this? It just seems like things like this keep happening to me." I was barely stable and was on the brink of a nervous breakdown. I needed comfort and needed it fast. Nothing so far cushioned my hard fall, not even my grandmother's tender loving.

"Jur mother called for ju today," she said softly. "She knows what happened. I told her everything."

I cried in her arms as I had done so many times before, and thought about my mom. It had been so long since I had seen her. I was sure she wondered why I had cut off all contact. My reasons were selfish, but I just didn't want to see her in jail anymore. No matter how many times she would put on her best cream and finest green outfit, which were the only colors they allowed her to wear, she couldn't fool me. I could tell she wasn't happy when I visited.

Both our feelings were torn apart every time we looked at each other. Her heart was severed from the fact that she hadn't raised me, and mine was crushed that her soul was so sad. I just thought it was best for us not to see each other anymore. Not once did I put myself in her shoes, thinking that maybe she needed just a piece of me, as opposed to nothing at all. I hated the choice I had made. For once, I shared her loneliness.

I kind of wished I could stay at my grandmother's overnight to catch one of her many phone calls, but I knew it wasn't safe. Besides, everything happens for a reason. Lord knows there was too much going on, and I wouldn't be able to bear anything else emotional.

"Oshyn, I have something to tell ju," she said, while pulling up a kitchen chair. At this point, there was nothing I wanted to hear, and by the sound of her voice, this wasn't going to be good.

"Please," I pleaded. "I'm not in the mood."

Grandma caressed my skin as she continued "There is something about Chloe, something about her mother that I think it's time for ju to know. Something that would explain their behaviors, why Mahogany did what she did to jur mother and Chloe to ju. I've never told ju this before, but now I think it's time for ju to know."

I sat up straight in my chair. She had successfully gotten my attention by getting ready to answer the questions I needed to know.

"Hey, Oshyn. Hey Grandma," Apples said, as she walked through the door. Micah and Bella weren't too far behind her playing tag.

My grandmother and I both looked at each other, knowing that our conversation would have to continue later on. Apples was family, but I could tell this was something Grandma didn't want to discuss with anyone else.

Apples caught a glimpse of my watery eyes and asked, "How are you doing?" I shrugged my shoulders, not quite sure how to answer her question. She left it alone.

Micah walked over to the kitchen TV and turned it on. I starred aimlessly at it as he flipped the channels looking for cartoons.

"STOP!" I yelled at him. "Turn it back!"

A picture of a woman caught my attention on the breaking news, a familiar one. It seemed like I had seen the face before. Everyone gathered around the television to see what I was talking about.

The news reporter stood aside as the camera focused in on a woman being carried out on a stretcher. The word shooting blinked across the screen. The familiar scene made me think of Chloe. Instantly, I pressed my hands over my ears, not believing what I'd done. *I really shot my cousin*, I thought. *What if she's dead?*

The house was beginning to close in on me, and I started to panic. I needed my space, and although they loved me, my family was starting to crowd me. I grabbed my keys and left out the house without saying a word. They noticed my sudden departure, and didn't say anything either. I was grateful.

I drove around town, not knowing where to go. Off a bridge at this point didn't sound too bad, but I knew that wasn't an option. Micah needed me, Grandma needed me, and hell, Apples needed me too. At that moment I realized what I needed. I needed to see my mother. I needed to make amends, before she was too old to forgive.

I found myself in front of *J.Kiss* steakhouse, where Brooklyn first captured my heart. I parked my car in front of the restaurant and watched the couples as they walked in, happy to be in love. I wanted to scream at the top of my lungs and warn the lovebirds about the dangers to come. I wanted to spare them the pain of the broken heart I'd endured, and let them know there was no such thing as love. Everything would be a lie.

I looked out the window and saw me and Brooklyn in those people. I watched how their faces lit up when the other was talking, and how close they held each other as they walked on the sidewalk. I saw how thankful they looked to be in each other's presence. I couldn't believe that I allowed myself to feel that way about Brooklyn and then have it all stolen away. *I knew it was too good to be true*, I said to myself, mad that I had fallen for him.

I couldn't take anymore of the torture I was putting myself through, so I decided to go back to the hotel. On my way there, I realized I hadn't given Micah a goodnight kiss in a while, and choose to go back to my grandmother's house for a quick moment. I needed to see my son and I thought it was only right to show my face and let her know that I was okay.

I got to the house and saw Apples and the kids in the living room knocked out. They were all watching a movie, but it looked like the movie had begun to watch them. I knew Apples like the back of my hand, and I wasn't surprised at all to still see her there. I knew she wasn't going anywhere until she knew I was safe. It was aggravating, but I appreciated it. I snuck past them and walked down the dark hall, peeking into my grandmother's room. She was reading her Bible with a dim light beside her.

"Hey, baby. Ju feel better now?" she said, never looking up. I jumped, kind of embarrassed that she knew I was staring at her.

"I don't know," I said, as I scratched my head. I didn't think I would ever feel better. "I want to thank you for everything, Mama, I really appreciate it."

"Come, give me hug," she told me, temporarily closing her Bible with her finger.

I walked over to her bed and laid my head on her lap. She ran her fingers through my hair as she always did, and hummed one of her gospel hymns. I closed my eyes and wept away all my hurts while she prayed for me.

She stopped suddenly and asked me, "Oshyn, is there something that jur not telling me?"

I lifted my head and wiped the snot from my nose. "No, I've told you everything," I said, assuring her that she knew about it all.

She pulled me closer to her, placing her hand on my stomach and whispered, "Jur pregnant, aren't ju?"

# 19

# CHLOE

I was out of it. The medication the doctor had me on made me feel like a zombie.

"Welcome back, Ms. Chloe," the old female nurse said to me, as she checked my vitals. Her accent reminded me of the islands, deep Jamaica.

"Where am I?" I asked, looking around, trying to figure out what century I was in.

"You're at Good Samaritan Medical Center, my dear, in Miami," she said, while she poked around my body, making sure everything was in order. She grabbed my hand in a mothering sort of way and said, "You've been out for a couple of weeks, sweetheart, and you're just waking up. Who did this to you?"

I moaned as I tried shifting positions in my bed.

"Don't move, honey, you'll just hurt yourself some more. Stay still and relax. Where is your family at?" she asked, with pen and paper in hand. "Give me a number so I can let them know what's happened to you and where you're at. I'm sure they are worried sick."

I ignored her attempt to help me, because as far as I was concerned, I had no family. It had been two weeks since I had been shot and no one had been to check on me. I know me and my grandmother have had our differences, but damn, I was still her granddaughter. Had I been Oshyn, she would have hunted me down and found me in rain, sleet, shine or snow. But instead, I was left abandoned once again.

I looked down at the bandages and panicked. "My baby. Is my baby okay?" I asked, rubbing my wounded stomach.

"I'm sorry sweetheart…you lost it," she said, in a way that let me know she had become accustomed to giving bad news.

"Why?" I cried to no one in particular. The nurse walked over to my bed and sat down beside me. She rubbed my unruly hair just like my grandmother always rubbed Oshyn's.

Those nights when we were younger, and she used to rebuke the demons out of me, were the same nights she rocked her precious Oshyn to sleep. That's when I learned that every shut eye ain't sleep. I knew she didn't think that I was smart enough to realize how different she treated the both of us, but I was and had been from the very beginning.

I sobbed uncontrollably because I lost my baby. I had

many abortions before, but this loss was different. Brooklyn was supposed to be mine and we were going to raise our child together. I had everything planned out, including the conception process. It was that night at the hotel when I returned to North Carolina. He showed up at my hotel room and I seduced him into bed with me. Shit had started getting so good that he forgot to put on a condom. We fucked over and over again until I was sure I was pregnant, and I was.

That's why I gave him a pass on his life while we were in Miami. Quon knew about the trip, and gave me specific orders to kill him while we were there, but I couldn't go through with it. I loved him and didn't want my child to grow up fatherless like I had. Now I had no child, and no man either.

My limp and groggy body stared out the window, while the medicine the nurse put in the IV slide through my veins. I knew whenever this stuff wore off, I'd be hit head on with the pain of everything. Right now I simply couldn't feel a thing. She talked to me some more, as I started dozing off again to relive the same childhood nightmare I had been having for weeks…

I asked my mom why she was getting so dressed up to do laundry as she zipped up her skintight party dress.

She called me princess as she explained to me that I had to look beautiful wherever I went. She pinned up her long, silky curly tresses and sprayed Channel No. 5

on her dress, never letting it touch her skin. "Don't like the way it taste," she would often say. I always wondered how she knew.

My mother, Mahogany, was so beautiful. And at eight years old, I worshipped the ground she walked on, wanting to be just like her when I grew up. She was more like a friend than a mother, letting me drink beers while she partied with her friends late at night.

My mother put the finishing touches on her makeup and put her knee high boots on before we headed out the door. *Man, she's pretty*, I thought to myself as I watched her sashay to the car, heels sinking into the slush. *The only time she looked this pretty was when she went to church, to the club, and when she did laundry.*

My Aunt Roslyn, had bought a brand new washer and dryer and my mother took full advantage. We did laundry often, at least three times a week. I often wondered why we washed so much when we didn't own that many clothes.

We always went to the house when Aunt Roslyn was at work. She was a registered nurse and worked long twelve-hour shifts. Mommy made sure Auntie wasn't around when she came over, because they always wound up arguing about something. We pulled up in the snow filled driveway and parked next to Uncle Rae's rusty blue pick-up truck. It looked like someone attempted to shovel the driveway and got tired halfway through. He opened the door and let us in, rubbing my head like I was a puppy, and his eyes never leaving my mother's cleavage.

"Hey, Uncle Rae," I said, anxious to get out of the cold and to my cartoons and Oshyn's toys. She always had the latest.

Uncle Rae was Oshyn's pretend daddy. Aunt Roslyn told her that her real one died when she was little. My mother told me the same thing about mine. Oshyn got a permanent replacement and I got a lot of temps.

If Rochester wasn't known for anything else, it was known for it's fifteen-degree days, and this was definitely one of them. I sat on the blue and brown plaid couch and turned on the TV. *The Smurfs* were on.

"Chloe, baby, remember not to bother Mommy and your Uncle while we do laundry, okay?" She reminded me as though I had forgotten the routine.

"Okay," I said.

I woke up to my Aunt Roslyn nudging me on my shoulder with Oshyn by her side. She was seven.

"Hey, Aunt Ros," I whispered rubbing my eyes. "Hey, Oshyn."

"Hi, Chloe," Oshyn said, waving her hand.

"I just came home to get something for work," she said, looking around frantically for something that was obviously important. "Where is your mother?" I guess she finally slowed down and realized I was in her house, even though I shouldn't have been.

"She's in the back doing laundry with Uncle Rae," I

answered clueless. Her face changed. Turned stone cold. She knew something that I didn't. The washer and dryer were in the room with me and always had been.

She got up and went directly for the coat closet, digging into a few shoeboxes until she found the one that she wanted. She pulled out a .357 magnum and headed to the back.

"Y'all stay here," she demanded. But curiosity got the best of me and I followed, with Oshyn tagging along.

"Mahogany? Rae..." my Aunt Roslyn said, wishing she was in a nightmare. "How could you?"

Lines of heroin covered the worn nightstand, and in all the excitement, no one saw the gun. My mother pulled the sky blue sheets over her big breasts. The stale smell of sex was in the air. They hadn't expected her back for another four hours.

"Let me explain," Rae said, as he slithered his way out the bed.

"How could you do this to me? You're my husband, my sister! How?" she screamed.

"It's not what you think," he said, hoping that she'd buy his story.

"It's not what she thinks?" screamed my mom. "Tell her! Tell her who you really want Rae. I can't do this anymore. I don't want to hide anymore... *TELL HER*!"

"What the fuck are you talking about?" my Aunt asked, befuddled.

"Me and Rae have been dealing for almost a year now

and..."

"SHUT UP!" Rae shouted, through his clenched teeth.

"No, *you* shut up! I'm sick of the lies." My mom's voice cracked. She tried to hold back the tears.

Everyone had forgotten about us. No one noticed that we were in the room, soaking up all the drama. Oshyn stood by my side crying. She was upset because of all the confusion. I held her hand.

"But you're my sister," Aunt Roslyn reminded my mother, as though she'd forgotten.

"Not by choice. You think you're better than everyone else cause you went to school. You think your shit don't stink. Well, you're not and it does, bitch. He don't want you no more."

Weak from the foul odor of deceit, Aunt Roslyn sat back, trying to figure out where it all went wrong. Was she supposed to feel bad for being the one to get out of the hood? Everyone had choices to make. She chose education and family. My mother chose party, men and drugs.

Both women were exceptionally beautiful with amazing bodies, but my mother just couldn't get the green-eyed monster off her back. She wanted everything that my aunt had, and since she couldn't get it, she opted to fuck her men. She'd had most of them, and all of us, including my aunt, knew.

Aunt Roslyn looked up, her face was more sad than

angry. She grinned and aimed the gun at my mother.

"You've betrayed me for the last time, bitch!"

She pulled the trigger, lodging one bullet in my mother's chest. I ran to her aid, barely able to see through my tear stained eyes. Oshyn ran to her mother.

"Mommy, please don't go!" I pleaded, as I watched her soul slip out of her body.

"Don't…be…like…me," she warned me, in between desperate attempts for air.

I placed my small hands over her heart where the bullet entered, and tried keeping the blood in. It was just so much and my hands were so little. My mother died in my arms, and any decency in me died that day with her.

My Uncle Rae tried calling the ambulance, in an attempt to save her life so my aunt wouldn't have to go to jail for murder, but it was too late. She was dead on arrival.

Sitting on the couch with a cigarette in her mouth, Aunt Roslyn rubbed the temple of her head with the murder weapon. Maybe she was contemplating suicide and chose not to because of Oshyn. The police swarmed the scene and handcuffed my aunt, reading her the Miranda rights in front of my dead mother.

As she was taken out, she turned around and looked at me. Without blinking, I stared back at her, wishing looks could kill. *This ain't over*, I thought, still staring into her swollen eyes, *this ain't over*!

## 20

# OSHYN

My grandmother's comment hit me like a ton of bricks. I don't know how she knows these things, but her intuition needed to start minding its own business. I told her that I was going to get an abortion, and she blew up. I had never seen her that upset before in my life. She wasn't in the baby killing business and didn't allow that type of talk in her home. I should have known better. I told her I couldn't handle it, but when she calmed down, she kept telling me that God doesn't give us more than we can bear. I couldn't tell, because at this point, I was barely able to blink.

I slept in her bed, and when morning came, I decided to get out the house, or risk becoming crazier than I was. So, I decided to go to work. Brian really stepped up and handled everything for me and I really appreciated the help. He didn't know what was going on. He thought I had a stomach virus that was contagious and I preferred it that way. I still didn't have the strength to explain to him in detail what was really going on.

"Hey, boss lady. What are you doing out?" he asked surprised. I had startled him with my presence. The office was surprisingly in perfect condition, and everything seemed to be running smooth. That put my conscious at ease.

"I just came to check on a few things, that's all. Everything looks great. How is business?"

"Ah, man, this shit is incredible. We're a month above schedule and the money is pouring in way faster than I had expected. I've already started on the Chandlers project which, I'm not sure if you remember, are the one hundred and ten unit town homes in Knightdale that the builders started breaking ground on."

"That's great," I said, staring out the oversized window, not really hearing anything he said.

"Oshyn, what's wrong? You look horrible and your eyes are red and puffy. You just don't look like yourself."

"Well thanks, Brian!" I said, trying to sound a bit happier. I had worn my shades out the house, but had forgotten not to take them off. "I told you that I had a stomach virus."

"Yeah, right! Something is going on that you're not telling me. Brooklyn has been by here looking for you, and it hasn't been just one day. He's been coming by everyday for two weeks. Now to me, that's a little suspicious, seeing as though he is your *husband!* Look,

Oshyn, I know you're my boss, but I consider you a friend too. If you need to talk…please talk to me."

I held my head down, wanting to unload everything on him. I wanted to pour out my past pains, hurts and my demons. I wanted to tell him how my *husband* and my cousin had been fucking each other the whole time, right under my nose.

I parted my lips to tell him everything when he said, "And there is this other man who has been coming around here too, asking a whole lot of questions."

Fear struck my body as I wondered if the police had found out about the attempted murder I committed. I started sweating, which was always an indication of my nervousness. My breathing got shallower and I suddenly felt out of control, as everything seemed to close in on me once again.

I took a seat fast before I hit the ground and asked, "Was it the police?"

"No, don't think so."

"What did he look like, what kind of questions was he asking?" I asked frantically, needing as much information as I could get.

"He was an older black guy and he looked very distinguished. I thought he was a potential investor, but the type of things he was asking just wasn't right. His body language was off, a little creepy even."

"Like what?" I asked, desperate for answers. I wanted him to give me something, anything.

"I don't know, Oshyn, it just wasn't right."

I let it go. Obviously he didn't know anything other than what he was telling me, or I would have known. I put my sunglasses back on and got up to leave.

"Thank you, Brian," I said, heading to the door.

"Oshyn, please tell me what's going on. Are you in trouble?"

I walked over to him and gave him a hug. I cupped his face in my sweaty hands, smiled and assured him, "Everything is fine, really." He wasn't buying it. "Look, I need a little more time off. I thought that I was ready to come back, but I'm not. It's too soon."

"Too soon for what?" he asked.

I ignored him and continued, "Can you hold the business down for me for another week maybe?"

"Yeah, of course, but…"

"And Brian," I interrupted, "please don't tell Brooklyn that you've seen me. And if the mystery man comes back around, please get a detailed description and find out specifically what he wants."

"Yeah, okay," he said, finally giving up. "Oh, wait, before I forget." He went to his office and came back with an envelope in his hand. "This is from Brooklyn. He asked me to give it to you whenever I saw you."

He tried handing it to me, but I just stared at it. Brooklyn had touched it, and I could faintly smell his scent all over it. I didn't want whatever it was in my possession for fear that it would supernaturally make him appear. I hated him for all that he had done, but I was still weak. I loved him. Brian pushed the envelope a little closer to me, and I took it from him reluctantly.

"Thank you, B," I said, giving him another tight hug. "You are my friend."

I rode around for a bit, going nowhere in particular. I wanted to be alone, lost in my own thoughts. Between the sleeping pills and the nausea, I hadn't had time to really reflect on what happened, and I wasn't quite sure that I wanted to. I drove around like a drunk driver, not being able to see through my tears. I drove to the movie theatre and parked the car. The envelope Brooklyn had for me rested on the dashboard. I stared at it like it was going to get up and walk away any minute now, before finally deciding to see what was inside.

I opened it and read what I knew were lies:

Oshyn,

I don't deserve to say your name, much less write you a letter, but I'm thankful that you are taking the time to read this. I have been by your job and your house everyday, with no luck of finding you. I just want to talk. I don't blame you at all for not wanting to see me, but I've been praying for a miracle. I just need one chance to explain myself to you, just one chance. I love you, I need you, I miss you and I'd do anything to feel your touch again. I wrote you a poem and hope that you can forgive me for what has happened.

As soon as I saw you
I knew you were the one
The twinkle of your eye
Let me know my search was done
You felt the same way
I could tell in your smile
You asked me never to hurt you
I made that promise to you out loud
Weeks went by and I wanted you in my life
Wasn't satisfied with you being my girl
So I asked you to be my wife
You agreed without hesitation
Making me the happiest man on earth
I promised to love, honor and cherish you
I vowed to make this thing work
Then you saw with your own eyes
The weakness of my lust
I broke your heart
And betrayed your trust
I committed the unspeakable
Something I wouldn't even forgive
I did the unthinkable
Something I don't want to relive
I want you to forgive me
I'm sorry for what I've done
I want to explain what happened
But I'd understand if you never come
I've made the biggest mistake of my life

*And I'm forever in debt*
*I promised God I'd take care of his daughter*
*A promise not kept*
*I love you baby and I'm sorry for hurting you. Please forgive*
*me.*

*Love for the rest of my life,*
*Brooklyn Jones*

I crumpled up the paper and threw it out the window. I knew it was a mistake to even read what he had to say, everything that was in there was all full of shit. This nigga fucks my cousin and then tries to make everything right with a corny ass poem. He could suck my ass as far as I was concerned. Brooklyn was supposed to be different. He promised that he would never tell me a lie and I believed him.

I wiped my face with my hand, realizing that the smell of his cologne was now on my skin. I was going to go back to my hotel to wash it off, but I was much closer to my grandmother's house. I needed this off me ASAP.

I headed straight for the shower as soon as I got inside the house.

"Hi to ju too," Grandma said, as she leaned on the bathroom door.

"Oh, hi Mama. Sorry I didn't speak first, I just needed to take a hot shower. I'll be out in a minute." I got out the shower, dried off, and put my clothes back on. I had to wait until I got back to the hotel to change them.

When I got out the bathroom, I found Grandma at the kitchen table reading the Bible.

"Don't you get tired of reading that thing?" I asked.

"Tired? Do ju get tired of breathing?" she snapped, not expecting a reply. "I didn't think so."

I sat down next to her and put my head down on the table. The running around had gotten me exhausted and I needed a nap.

"Oshyn, the other day I was trying to tell ju something about Chloe and her mother and I wasn't able to finish."

I lifted up my head, wanting her to get it over with, and asked, "What is it?"

"There is no easy way to tell ju this, so I'll just come out and tell ju." I saw the fear in her eyes. She was scared to death about whatever it was she was getting ready to unveil. "Mahogany is jur real mom," she said, grasping her Bible for dear life.

"Mahogany who?" I asked, not understanding what she was trying to tell me.

"Jur Aunt Mahogany is jur real mother, not Roslyn. She was raped by one of her johns and didn't want to keep ju. Jur mother pleaded with her to spare jur life and promised that she'd cared for ju forever. She told her that she'd never tell ju what happened, and for the rest of jur life you'd think of her as only jur aunt."

I stared at her with my mouth wide open. *So much*

*for God giving us no more than we can bear*, I thought, as I tried picking my face up off the floor.

"So, I'm a rape baby? My father is a rapist?" Surprisingly, I didn't shed a tear. Maybe I was just in shock, but I had no more tears left in me. I was all dried up.

"No! Ju are a child of God, and loved more than any child I know. We did everything we could so ju would never feel out of place. That's why there will be no talk of killing my grandchild that rests in jur stomach. We will raise that baby up in love and in truth. If it were up to me, I would have never told ju, but jur mother thought it best for ju to know. She didn't want to be held accountable to God for living a lie."

She stopped talking for a brief second to see if I had anything to say. I was speechless. "Even though Chloe and ju came from the same mother, ju turned out differently. I showed ju so much love to shield ju from the truth that I forgot about Chloe. I blame a lot her behavior on me. If I had showed her half of what ju got, she wouldn't have turned out like this."

"Is she dying?" I asked, curious to know why my mother felt the need for a sudden confession.

"I don't know? She wouldn't tell me anything. She sounds different though, like something is wrong. All she wants to do is talk to ju."

"You don't know? It seems like you know everything else, and you can't figure out if my mom, who's really my aunt, is dying or not?"

I was angry. Who I thought I was, was not who I am. I had been told a lie my whole life, and was now a stranger to myself.

My grandmother did her best to calm me down, but I didn't want to hear nothing she had to say. While she was still talking, I got out the chair, knocking it to the floor, and stormed out the house. There was nothing else she could say that I wanted to hear.

# 21

# CHLOE

I kept having those reoccurring nightmares, the one when my mother was murdered. I was sure the visions would end once I got out the hospital, but they continued, even while I recovered at Joy's townhouse.

The hospital released me about a month ago, and from there I remembered being angry that I had to catch a cab to the airport. No one was even there to welcome me back to the real world, not Grandma, not Beef, and not even Brooklyn. He was the reason I'd been shot.

Joy agreed to pick me up from the airport, and seemed to be the only one who cared for me. She continuously asked questions about what happened to me, and got frustrated when I wouldn't answer. She was cool, but I didn't want her thinking there was anything special between us just because everyone else dissed the hell out of me.

Beef, I know, had moved on, and there was no point

in trying to reconcile our relationship. It was, without a doubt, over and for the best. I contemplated getting all my money together and moving far away from Raleigh, never to return again, but what I had to settle was much more important.

Revenge was a far better reward for what Oshyn had done to me. My baby was dead and Oshyn was responsible. I knew in my heart it was Brooklyn's baby, and that reason alone, made my decision more justifiable. Oshyn needed to be held accountable for all the things that she and her mother had done in my life.

The doctor told me that the bullet came inches from hitting my spine, but missed. It didn't puncture anything major and, therefore, he expected my recovery to be speedy. *Nothing major*, I repeated in my head, as I wondered about the baby I had miscarried. He said the injuries were minor, but I know the psychological damage it had done to my mind was much worse.

I had been hearing voices from my mother lately, asking me why I let her die. I would talk back to her, reminding her there was nothing I could've done. I was only eight years old and I didn't know what was going on, but she insisted on blaming it on me.

I tried getting her accusatory voice out of my head, but it only got louder, to the point where I couldn't hear anything else. "Oshyn has really done something for herself. Her office is beautiful, I'm really proud of her," the deep voice said, startling me. I couldn't figure out if it was my mother speaking to me in spirit, or if someone was really standing before me.

I thought I had the house to myself, at least until Joy got back from the mall. I turned around and silently observed him standing next to the door, unloosing his tie. The briefcase that he had placed near the coat rack made his appearance look like one that should've been on Wall Street. He was a handsome man. Always had been, but violent as hell.

"Why the fuck do you keep going there? Stick to the fucking plan before you ruin everything," I said to Quon, frustrated at his defiance. I wasn't shocked though, after all, this was the nigga that stuck his gun up my pussy.

"Chloe," he said, sounding like a patient parent. "I'm going to let what you just said slide because of the medications you've been taking, but one more outburst like that and I will kill you, do you understand?"

I rolled my eyes and pouted like the child he thought he was talking to. I had already been shot in the stomach, and didn't want any other injuries from this lunatic.

Quon had become impatient with my handling of Brooklyn. He wanted Brooklyn dead! And he wanted Apples and Bella in his possession a lot faster than what I was producing, so he decided to fly from Rochester to NC to handle it himself. The postcard arrived to let me know that he was coming. It was a simple black and white flick of an old woman smelling a rose. On the back it read, *I'll be there soon.* He knew to send it to Joy's house because that was the only address I had given him to contact me. He came to settle the score and nothing else.

Joy walked in with both hands filled with bags and rolled her eyes at the sight of the both of us. She was still mad at me for not telling her what happened in Miami, so our communication had become real scarce.

"You straight?" she asked sarcastically.

I looked at her and returned the eye gesture, knowing that she could care less about my well-being. I almost didn't want to eat the food she had prepared, thinking that she was mad enough to poison me. I guess I can't blame her, though. I was laid up in her house wounded, and wouldn't tell her why.

Quon took a seat on the leather couch adjacent to me. He and Joy never acknowledged each other. She was mad that he'd made himself comfortable in *her* home with *my* permission. She didn't know him or want him in her house, and he simply didn't give a fuck. He, on one occasion, dared her to make him leave. I interfered with the argument, telling her to leave it alone for fear that he would hurt her. She left it alone.

"So, what's good with the plan?" Quon asked, ready to get the ball rolling. "I see you up and moving now, and I'm ready to get my family back. Time is ticking and I need to be out of here as soon as possible."

"Just give me one more week, and I'll have enough strength to make it happen."

He took a deep breath, showing his extreme impatience and disappointment. He hadn't planned on being here for more than a week, and his trip now was being extended to two.

"Well, let's run through the plan again," he demanded, wanting to make sure I had everything perfectly planned. He made little to no room for mistakes, and wanted everything to be just right.

"I still have a spare key to Oshyn's house, and that's what we're going to use to get in. That way, it won't have to look like a break in. Apples still goes there on certain days to do laundry while the kids are at my grandmother's house, so you can make your move then."

I was still confused to what he was going to do after he got her, but at that point, my job was done. She was out of my hands and into his. I just wanted him out the state so that I could sleep easier.

"Why don't y'all just leave the girl alone? She don't bother nobody, and your hating ass is always fucking with her," Joy said, referring to the plot against Apples. "Who is this punk ass nigga anyway?" she asked, pointing to Quon. "Oshyn is your cousin, and you sit here and talk about breaking into her house for him? I don't give a fuck who you are," she said, redirecting her conversation to Quon. "Get the fuck out my house!"

They stared at each other like two pit bulls in an

intimate scenario of whose life was going to end first. Joy shocked me standing her position. She stood in the middle of the living room with her hands on her hips and waited for his next move.

"Okay," Quon said, with his hands up in surrender position. "You win."

I stared at him suspiciously, while he got up and walked over to his neatly packed bags. I thought he had obsessive-compulsive disorder, the way he kept everything sparkling clean and in perfect order. If it weren't for his evil ways, he would've been the ideal houseguest.

He bent down to pick up his bags and came back up with a gun attached to a silencer. I shrieked, startling Joy, whose back was facing Quon. She turned around facing the last second of her life as he pulled the trigger. Joy fell to the floor, with a gunshot in the middle of her forehead. Her spiritless eyes stared into mine, wondering why I didn't help. I had no answers.

"Change of plans. Tomorrow is the day that I'll be reunited with my love," he said poetically, as if he hadn't just committed a murder.

Quon carefully put the gun back into his bags and grabbed Joy off the floor. That was the last time I saw her. Death was so familiar, I couldn't shed a tear.

## 22

# CHLOE

"I think we should come back another day. It looks like no one has been here in a while," I suggested to Quon, as we walked around the house investigating it critically.

When we came in, all the shades were drawn, and it looked like Oshyn hadn't been around in weeks. I knew by the dust on her TV stand and the picture frames that she had been missing for a minute. If there was one thing that bothered her, it was a dirty house, and hers was always spotless. Everything was in its specific place, making her crib look more like a model home than one a family actually lived in.

"We're going to stay until she gets here. I don't care if it takes days, we're not leaving." His mind was set in stone, and I knew there was no changing it. He kept his black leather gloves on, not wanting to attract any added attention to himself. It was all for precaution, just in case the police came to fingerprint the scene his existence would never come up.

We waited in the family room, admiring Oshyn's prized wall of pictures that she cherished so dearly. Quon paid especially close attention to the flick with his beloved Apples and Bella. He took it off the wall to examine it more closely, probably dreaming about the life that could have been, the life of love they once had. I left him in a maze of his own thoughts and excused myself to the bathroom. I just didn't want to be around while he reminisced about the past.

I made it to the hallway bathroom not far from where Quon was, and changed my pad that was filled with the remnants of my dead baby. I was still bleeding pretty heavily from the miscarriage. I went to throw the pad away in the small trashcan when I saw something I shouldn't have. I picked up the rectangular box and read the label, EPT, out loud. I shook it around and realized there was something still inside. *She had been home.* I thought about Oshyn while I grabbed the white stick that indicated whether she was pregnant or not.

Positive.

My heart dropped to the bottom of my shoe. I took a seat on the lid of the toilet and clenched my stomach that started to cramp again. I lifted up my shirt to check the bandage that covered my bullet wound, and saw that it was leaking. I had been doing too much lately and I wasn't allowing my body to properly heal. Quon had me feeling more like a hostage than a partner, and hadn't given me too much of a choice on anything. It was either his way or death, literally.

I stared at the pregnancy test stick closely one last time, hoping somehow to change the results. *This cant be*, I said to myself, wondering why she was pregnant and I wasn't.

*"Chloe,"* I heard a voice sing. I looked around, trying to figure out who was talking to me. *"It's your mother baby,"* she said, in a tender loving way.

"Ma?" I asked, making sure I wasn't tripping.

*"Yes, dear, it's me."*

"How could she, Ma?" I asked, as I broke out into tears. "I loved him. How come she can be pregnant with his baby and kill mine?" I held my head in my hands and cried hard.

*"Baby, don't cry. That little bitch will get what she deserves."* For some reason, those words didn't soothe me and my mother could sense it. *"Chloe, snap out of it and do as I say,"* she said, followed by a list of instructions she gave me and wanted me to follow step by step.

When I heard the last command, I thought damn, *ruthless*. I nodded, showing that I agreed, and went back out to sit with Quon in the living room. For some reason, I felt safer with him in my view.

There was something unusual about him. On his forehead were tiny beads of sweat that were growing by the second. That wasn't normal for him. Even when he killed Joy, his face was as dry as the desert, but this, the perspiration indicated something different. He looked up at me and smiled. His eyes were red and glossy, and his dry mouth was covered with crust all around it. *He looked normal when I went in the bathroom*, I thought, as I tried to figure out how long it had taken me to come out. It looked like I was staring into the face of the devil. I started to believe that he was.

He was getting ready to say something to me when we heard the keys in the door jingling. The room was still dark and everything was in place, except for the pictures he refused to put back. Apples walked in the house, leaving the front door cracked a bit. It looked like she had been grocery shopping and left the door open to get the rest of the bags out of the car.

She walked over to one of the windows and rotated the blinds so they would allow the sunlight to saturate the room. Once the rays hit her face, she blocked it with her hands and turned around to avoid any more heat, bumping into Quon. He had crept up behind her without her knowledge.

Her hand clenched her heart as she gasped for air. The light pink velour pants she wore revealed the pee that ran down her legs. She was staring the grim reaper dead in the face, and she knew it.

"Hey, Apples," I said, walking out the cut, making my presence known. "Look who I found for you!"

Her breathing got a little heavier and her face turned

pale white.

"Hey, baby, I've been looking all over for you," Quon said, as he gently placed her hand in his. She tried to snatch it away, but his grip had tightened, making her squirm from the pain. She gave up when she saw the gun he was toting pointing in her direction.

"Please," she whimpered, like a dying dog, "let me go."

Her cries fell on deaf ears as Quon kissed her terrified face. She struggled to free herself from him once more, but he refused to loosen the hold he had on her. He promised himself that he would never lose her again, and it started the second he laid his eyes on her.

Everyone's thoughts were interrupted by the sudden sound of people running toward the door. No one saw that it was still open until it was too late. Quon, not thinking twice, opened fire on the intruders until he was sure no one was moving.

"Noooo!" Apples screamed, as she broke away from him.

Before she could reach the door, he stopped her in her tracks by lodging a bullet in her back. She fell flat on her face, screaming in pain and still reaching for the door. I ran to the door to see what damage had been done and to who. I almost passed out at what I saw.

"Micah!" I yelled, as I threw my body on top of his.

He fought to hang on to every breath he took, but his lungs appeared to be giving up. I looked directly into his eyes and could tell he was hurt pretty badly. A few feet away, Bella laid on the ground also, struggling to stay alive. I wasn't sure where they were hit, but clearly an ambulance was needed, but Quon's expression said *no*. *They weren't suppose to be here*, I thought, as I blamed myself for letting this happen. *They were supposed to be at Grandma's.* The kids weren't part of the plan. They weren't supposed to get hurt, they had nothing to do with this.

Calling for help was out of the question, so I hoped they held on until I could get them to safety. I looked around, trying to find Apples who had seemed to disappear. *She couldn't have gone far,* I thought, picturing her move around with the hole in her back. I noticed that Quon was now gone too. I quietly followed the blood trail from the living room to the hallway and was disgusted at what I saw.

Quon was on top of Apples, ramming his dick inside of her while she lay dead. All her lifeless body could do was jerk back and forth as he thrust himself into her. Without him noticing, I grabbed the gun from the floor next to him. He never stopped his motion, never even slowed down to see what I was doing. I think he expected to die and figured this was the best way to go out. He had become senile and needed to be put down. At this point, it was kill or be killed.

I lifted the gun up and pulled the trigger, shooting him near his heart. He cried out in pain at the unexpected bullet that was now lodged in his chest. He pressed his hand close against his chest and turned to me with murder in his eyes. Instantly, I got chills after listening to his unstable breathing pattern. Sometimes I'd feel better if he talked, screamed even, but he never said a word. I didn't want him dead, not yet, I just needed to slow him down so that I'd have control again. I still had big plans for him and needed him around. I looked back at him lying on the floor with his eyes still glued to me. I ignored his attempt to fill my body with fear and walked away. He had a way of intimidating people even when he was helpless. With no other place to go, I decided to watch Quon die and wait for Oshyn. She had to come through here sooner or later, and I wanted to be the first person she saw when she got here.

# 23

# OSHYN

Shadows don't usually scare me, but tonight they did. It was something about the way they stared at me that just didn't sit well in my stomach. I didn't trust them, at least not for the night.

The rain poured down hard on my flesh as I stood in my driveway, causing my hair to frizz up. It didn't matter though, I desperately needed it. I needed to be baptized by nature and confess for all the wrongs I'd done, but it was too late. At this point, even I couldn't forgive me.

The full moon beamed down on my face, soaking it with its uncertainty. Even it was oblivious to what the night held. No one knew that I was coming home, and I preferred it that way. I needed to spend some time in solitude to reflect on my life. I needed to restore what I had lost. I needed a night of restoration.

I walked into my home, locking the door behind me. The air was thick, making it hard to breath. I flipped on the lights only to be greeted by the same darkness that I had arrived to. *Maybe the thunderstorm kicked out the electricity*, I tried to convince myself. I felt my way over to the fuse box, located in the living room, using the wall as my cane.

"What the hell?" I said, as I tripped over something, losing my balance and falling face first onto the hardwood floor.

I thought for sure I knew my house inside and out in the dark. *Must've been something Micah left out*, I assured myself. I pulled myself up, using my cold Italian leather couch as leverage. I finally reached the fuse box, turning on the lights, only to see what it was I tripped over…

I screamed to the top of my lungs like I was in a horror film. There before me was my best friend on the floor with a puddle of blood underneath her. Her pants were off and the foul stench that came from her made me turn my head.

"Apples! Apples, get up!" I pleaded with her to open her eyes but it was too late. My hands were covered in blood from falling on her and I didn't know what to do. My hands trembled as I tried to find my cell phone in a pocketbook that was too big. Finally finding it, I tried getting a steady grip. "Apples baby hold on, I'm a get you some help!" I assured her, refusing to acknowledge the fact that she was long gone. Just then, I looked over, only to see Quon laid flat on the floor a few yards away. I got it together and dialed *91*…

❈ ❈ ❈

"Welcome home, sleepy head," Chloe said, to me as I came to.

I thought that maybe I was having a bad dream, but soon concluded that it was all real. The way my head was pounding, it felt like it had been beat in with a baseball bat. I touched where it hurt the most, only to find blood on my fingertips. I had been hit with something, but I couldn't figure out what it was. I wasn't even sure what had happened or how long I was out for.

"Oshyn!" Chloe screamed, making my headache that much worse.

I looked up and saw her sitting on my coffee table with a gun in her hand. It took a couple of minutes for my vision to clear and when it did, I surveyed the room and saw Micah and Bella sprawled out on the floor covered in blood.

"Don't move," she said, pointing the gun at me as I ran to their side. I ignored her threat. "They were just an accident, I promise," she said, without emotion.

"Why?" I cried, while the tears streamed down my face. "Micah, baby, Mommy is here…wake up, please!" I pleaded with him to open his eyes, as his blood covered me.

"The kids were an accident, Oshyn," she repeated, while she paced the floor. "No one was supposed to die."

"Who else did you hurt?" I asked, looking up at her slowly.

"That's it. Apples and Quon are dead," she said, with satisfaction. "But don't worry, you're well equipped to make a new family!"

"What are you talking about?" I asked, crying and caressing Micah in my arms.

She held up the pregnancy test I took last night and waved it in the air. "Congratulations," she said, with an evil smile on her face. "You're having a new baby!" Suddenly her smile faded away just as quickly as it came, and she started rubbing her stomach where she had been shot. She cocked her head sideways and locked her cold eyes with mine. "I was having a baby too and you took it from me. You and your bitch-ass mother took everything from me." She smiled again, wiping the sweat off her face with the gun still in place. "Brooklyn wanted so badly to be a dad. He worked so hard to get me pregnant. I mean we damn near fucked every time we…"

I jumped off the floor and lunged toward her at full speed, catching her off guard. The gun fell out of Chloe's hand as I knocked her off the coffee table. She squirmed around, trying to get a hold of the weapon that was only a few inches away and succeeded. She quickly turned over to her back and there I was standing over her. I stared down the barrel of the gun determined that it wasn't my time to die. Without thinking twice, I kicked her forcefully in the chest. She lost the weapon again in an attempt to roll up in a fetal position. I quickly grabbed the gun and took my place back over her. Now it was Chloe, who was staring down the barrel of the gun, this time for good. Pulling the trigger and ending her life was supposed to be easy, but I struggled. She was my sister and I couldn't be responsible for her death. As much as I wanted her to stop breathing, my trigger finger wouldn't move. I put my head in my hands and started to cry. I wondered if Chloe knew the truth, that we shared the same womb, that my mother was Mahogany too. My head stayed in my hands as I contemplated what to do. Micah and Bella needed help, Apples needed help, we all needed help, and I was the only person that could do it for them. When I opened my eyes to grab my phone, Chloe had built up enough strength to kick me in my pussy, making the gun fall to the floor once again. She grabbed a hold of it and smiled.

Chloe raised her gun to me for the last time, and right when I was going to strike, pulled the trigger. I looked down, pressing both my hands on my stomach. My breathing got shallower as I watched my blood slip between my fingers.

All I saw was black all over again.

# 24

# *CHLOE*

KNOCK! KNOCK! KNOCK! Oh Shit! Somebody was knocking at the door like the police. I didn't see any lights, couldn't hear any sirens. A flashy silver ride sat outside the front door.

I dropped down to the floor to avoid being seen by whoever it was knocking at the door. With all the gunshots that had been fired, I was sure that the police had been called, but maybe I was wrong.

KNOCK! KNOCK! KNOCK! The knocks became louder.

"Oshyn, I just want to talk to you. Please just open the door," Brooklyn said, refusing to leave.

His keys rattled as he opened the door, only to be stopped by the chain that I had put up. I debated in my mind on whether to let him in or not. He wasn't part of the plan anymore, or was he? With Quon out of the picture, I had the option of letting him live. I looked over at Quon, not sure if he'd taken his last breath yet. My mind raced a mile a minute, trying to figure out what to do next.

"Oshyn, just hear me out and let me explain," he pleaded, with the little space he had that was separating him from the inside. "I love you."

I peeked at Oshyn, who was barley conscious and decided to let him in. He was, after all, the father of *my dead* child. I crept to the door and placed myself behind it, closing it shut to remove the chain. Slowly I re-opened the door.

"Oshyn?" he asked, wondering why no one was at the front door. "Oshyn?" he said, again this time coming in.

When he walked in far enough, I slammed the door shut behind him. His reflexes kicked in, spinning him around to see what was going on.

"Hey, daddy! I'm glad that you could join us," I said, showing him all the company that we had.

"What the fuck! Oshyn…," he said, trying to get by her side.

"Ah, ah, ah, not so fast. Have a seat and stay awhile!" I said, waving the gun in the direction I wanted him to go.

"Brooklyn. Help us," Oshyn whispered to him, as she desperately tried to hold on to what little life she had left.

"Oshyn, I'm so glad you're awake because Brooklyn has something that he wants to tell you." I looked at him and patiently waited for him to unload the truth to her.

The real reason he was here, his true motive.

"What are you talking about?" he said defiantly. He was sure that no one knew of his secret except for Quon, and he was dead.

"What am I talking about? Don't act stupid! I'm talking about Quon paying you to come here and kidnap Apples and Bella and bring them back to him. He told me everything!"

"Oshyn, she's lying, don't believe her," he said, trying to defend what little reputation he had left.

Oshyn nodded out, resembling a fiend that was high on dope. She stayed there for a second, but quickly came back, afraid that if she went to sleep she might not have woken up.

"Chloe," Brooklyn whispered, trying not to disturb Oshyn. "Fuck her, yo! Fuck all this shit! You're the one I really want," he added, having a sudden change of heart. "Let's just leave them here and run away, just me and you!"

"But she killed our baby, Brooklyn! She stole our family away from us."

"Then let me kill her," he offered, extending his hand toward the gun.

"Yeah, kill her and that fuck ass baby she's having," I said, happy with the plan.

"Huh?" he asked confused. "Baby, what baby?"

"Oh, she didn't tell you that she was pregnant? I saw the test in her bathroom!"

I watched him while he looked at Oshyn and slowly dropped his eyes down to her wounded stomach. The stare he gave her was intimate, letting me know that he loved her still. I snapped out the fantasyland I was in and realized that it was all bullshit. He was playing me for a fool, and for a minute, I fell for it.

"Don't worry about anything though," I said, playing along with his game. "I'm going to shoot that bitch dead in her stomach and kill them both off." I pointed the gun at her and was ready to pull the trigger.

"Wait!" he said, with his arms stretched out to me. "Give me the gun and let me do it. Let me kill her."

"Back up!" I said to him, as he came closer to me.

"I thought that we were on the same side? I love you!"

He was close enough for me to be able to smell the sweet scent of seduction on his skin. He reached in to touch my hair and I closed my eyes, as he lightly wrapped his fingers around my curls. Before I knew it, he had a fist full of my hair wrapped in his hands and shoved my face into the wall. The gun flew out of my hand as I grabbed my nose, which felt like it was broken.

I thought quickly, grabbing the knife I had in my pocket. I threw myself on top of him, swinging aimlessly like I had nothing to lose. My eyes watered so badly, I could barely see. As much as I fought him, my inability to see eventually caused a problem. As I clutched my knife, ready to slice, Brooklyn found the gun, and with the last bullet left...

## <u>ONE YEAR LATER</u>

I wish I could turn back the hands of time and start all over again. If I could, things would be a lot different. They say what goes around comes around, but I didn't do anything to deserve this. So many people I love are now dead, and I'm trying to pick up what pieces of my life are left. Grandma died weeks after the tragedy, and even though I was sad, I wasn't surprised. Her heart had been burdened with grief her whole life, and I knew she couldn't take anymore.

So now it's just Bella, my newborn son, and me. I named him Mye Storie. I almost named him Micah after his older brother, but I wanted him to have his own identity. He deserved that much. For some strange reason both me and Bella received an extra blessing from the Lord. Even though we were both shot with life threatening injuries, we survived, and my baby did too.

I moved out the graveyard that was once called home and found another place to live. My business, still going strong, has been ranked one of the top real estate companies in the region. I credited all the success to Brian. He stayed by my side through all the madness, refusing to leave. That's why when he finally decided to get married to his girlfriend, I was right by his side.

Brooklyn comes through often to see his son and tries to reconcile with me, but I can't, my heart is dead. I buried it with my first born and best friend. He does whatever he can to see what I'm feeling, but I'm blank. He calls me Oshyn Jones, I ignore him. He tries to give me money, I won't take it. Rumor has it that he opened up an account for Mye, that he can't get until he turns twenty-one. He put a million dollars in there for him, and refuses to tell me anything about the money.

The last time he came over, I told him he'd fucked my *sister* and not my cousin. He couldn't live with himself. That was the last time I saw him.

Whenever I look into my son's gray eyes, I think of him. I'm not sure if I could ever trust again, but only time will tell.

It's still not clear what happened to Chloe. I passed out after hearing all of the gun shots. Brooklyn said that he killed her, but when I came to, she was nowhere to be found. I never bothered asking the police because a part of me wanted her alive, and the other part wanted her dead. I bought a grave and a tombstone with her name on it and it still lies empty today. I guess I hope one day she will occupy it permanently.

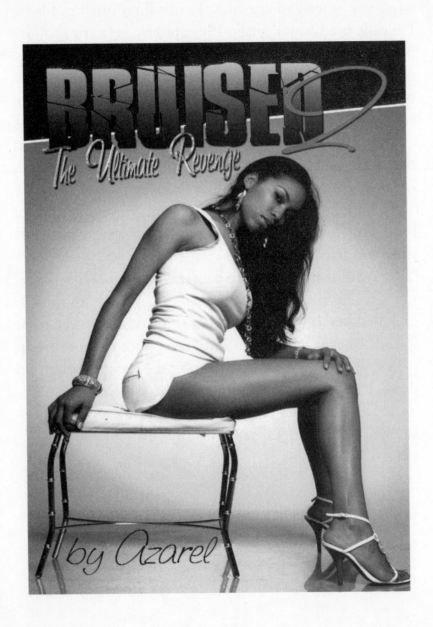

# Life Changing Books Order Form

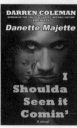    

Add $3.95 for shipping. Total of $18.95 per book. For orders being shipped directly to prisons Life Changing Books deducts 25%. <u>Cost are as follows,</u> $11.25 plus shipping for a total of $15.20.

Make money order payable to <u>Life Changing Books</u>. Only certified or government issued checks.

**Send to:**
**Life Changing Books/Orders P.O. Box 423**
**Brandywine, MD 20613**

**Purchaser Information**

Name _____

Register #_____
      **(Applies if incarcerated)**

Address_____

City_____

State/Zip_____

Which Books _____

# of books _____

Total enclosed  $_____

# Nvision Publishing Books Order Form

Add $3.95 for shipping. Total of $18.95 per book. For orders being shipped directly to prisons Life Changing Books deducts 25%. <u>Cost are as follows,</u> $11.25 plus shipping for a total of $15.20.

Make money order payable to <u>Life Changing Books</u>. Only certified or government issued checks.

**Send to:**
**Life Changing Books/Orders P.O. Box 423**
**Brandywine, MD 20613**

**Purchaser Information**

**Name** _____

**Register #** _____
**(applies if incarcerated)**

**Address** _____

**City** _____

**State/Zip** _____

**Which books** _____

**Number of Books** _____

**Total Enclosed  $** _____

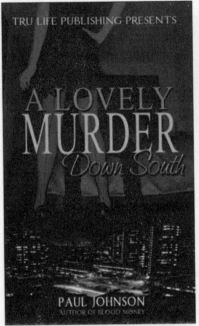

TRU LIFE PUBLISHING PRESENTS

A LOVELY
MURDER
*Down South*

PAUL JOHNSON
AUTHOR OF BLOOD MONEY

DARREN COLEMAN
author of the urban classic 'Do or Die'
presents

*Fast Lane*
a novel

by Eyone Williams

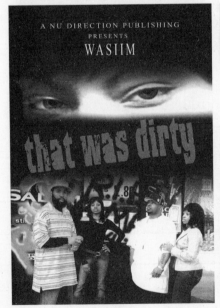

A NU DIRECTION PUBLISHING
PRESENTS
WASIIM

that was dirty

CRIME SCEN

Young
Assassin
By Mike G